PUFFIN BOOKS

WILLOW AND TWIG

JEAN LITTLE is the author of thirty books for children, including *Mama's Going to Buy You a Mockingbird*, *Different Dragons*, *Lost and Found* and *I Know an Old laddie*. She has won many awards for her work around the world, and her books have been translated into French, German, Dutch, Danish, Norwegian, Greek and Japanese. Jean Little lives on a farmstead near Elora, Ontario, with her sister, her niece and nephew, and a motley crew of animals.

D1232610

Willow and Twig

Jean Little

Puffin Books

PUFFIN BOOKS

Published by the Penguin Group

Penguin Books Canada Ltd, 10 Alcorn Avenue, Toronto, Ontario, Canada M4V 3B2

Penguin Books Ltd, 80 Strand, London WC2R 0RL, England

Penguin Putnam Inc., 375 Hudson Street, New York, New York 10014, U.S.A.

Penguin Books Australia Ltd, 250 Camberwell Road, Camberwell, Victoria 3124,
Australia

Penguin Books (NZ) Ltd, cnr Rosedale and Airborne Roads, Albany, Auckland 1310,
New Zealand

Penguin Books Ltd, Registered Offices: Harmondsworth, Middlesex, England

First published in Viking by Penguin Books Canada Limited, 2000
Published in Puffin Books, 2001

3   5   7   9   10   8   6   4

NATIONAL LIBRARY OF CANADA CATALOGUING IN PUBLICATION DATA

Little, Jean, 1932–
Willow and Twig

ISBN 0-14-130669-6

I. Title.

PS8523.I77W54 2001   jC813'.54   C2001-902677-3
PZ7.L7225Wi 2001

Visit Penguin Canada's website at **www.penguin.ca**

This story is for Sarah, who was not Angel,
Jeanie, who is definitely not Willow,
Ben, who was never Twig,
and Pat, who is daily Gram,
with my heart's love.

The schools Willow and Twig attend are real schools but the children themselves and all the other characters are imaginary. Stonecrop is the house in which I live: Ritz, my Seeing Eye dog, I have renamed Sirius since he is both a dog and a star. Tiggy and Panda, now dead, lived here when I began to write the story. Toby, my darling boy, is still very much alive. The manuscript written by Elspet Gordon and read by Willow can be found in my novel *The Belonging Place*.

Contents

Willow
and Twig

1
Nobody's Children

Willow did not let go of Twig until he pulled free. She was walking along with his hand in hers but with her mind busy telling Red Mouse why she wanted to go to school. Her small brother jerked away and ran when they were next to a muddy vacant lot between a run-down corner store and a boarded-up laundromat. Twig tore over to a patch of unkempt grass next to the empty building.

"Go after him, girl," Red Mouse said, inside her head.

Willow didn't need to be told. The moment Twig took off, she was in hot pursuit.

But the four-year-old stopped by some ragged weeds and squatted down. Willow watched him reach for something. Then she, too, saw the kitten.

"Is it dead?" she asked, although she knew Twig would not answer. Even if he had heard, "dead" was not one of his words.

It was almost dead. Its small, sharp bones stuck out

through its matted fur and it did not mew. Willow could hear it breathing though, short, raspy wheezes which told her it was very ill. Twig did not hear the laboured breathing but he felt the kitten shudder as he stroked it. His stubby hands, so apt to knock things over and strike people, touched the rough black fur so gently that Willow was reminded of butterfly kisses someone had given her once. Who?

"Twig, leave it," she said, knowing her brother wouldn't.

Twig rose, cradling the kitten's tiny bundle of bones close to his chest, and, with Willow hovering over him, carried it all the way back down the street and up the shabby stairs to Maisie's room.

"Put it back where you found it," Maisie said stonily, her light blue eyes not meeting theirs.

"But Maisie, it's starving," Willow pleaded. She knew that it was useless, that Maisie's order made sense, but she still needed to try to change the old woman's mind.

"So are we," snapped Maisie. "Maybe someone who can feed it will take it in. I can't keep us fed, let alone a half-dead kitten."

Her thin face was set. She turned her back on Twig and his small wheezing burden and pretended to be busy with something on the table. Willow, her heart heavy with a rage which she knew solved nothing, grabbed her brother's elbow and pushed him out the door.

"Wo?" Twig said, but without hope. Although he had been unable to take in Maisie's harsh words, he had read her unyielding look.

"Come on," Willow growled, her hand urging the small boy out the front door of the ramshackle building.

Why, she asked inwardly, why did her brother always make hard days harder? Why had he noticed the stupid cat? Why were the two of them so alone? Why wasn't Red Mouse, who had magic powers and could grant wishes, real and on hand when he was needed?

I'm not Supermouse, Red Mouse apologized. I would be if I could be, but I can't be what I'm not.

Willow would have smiled at his answer if she had not felt so desperate. She made herself relax her grip on Twig's arm. She must not let her brother guess the anger and confusion and helplessness roaring through her. Her strength was all the two of them had. Under her palm, she felt the tension in her little brother's muscles ease. His big brown eyes, raised for a second to her face, waited for her to fix things.

"Maybe we can find someone to take him," she said. Weakly.

Possible, Red Mouse murmured. But highly unlikely.

Shut up, mouse, Willow snapped at him.

The Jones children walked side by side down the street seeking for someone who looked soft-hearted enough to save a starving kitten. It was useless. With night coming on and a chill rain beginning, the street was empty. Anyway, nobody in his right mind would have wanted that particular cat.

Then, just as Willow was trying to decide what to do next, the kitten twitched violently and died without ever having made a cry. Twig dropped it, his eyes stretching wide with horror. Willow's hands shot out to catch it as it fell.

What now? She asked Red Mouse.

I suggest burial, he said. It's your only viable option.

Willow wondered, not for the first time, where her

imaginary mouse had picked up his voice. It was not small and squeaky but grown-up and kindly with laughter in it. His language was adult too. He was not only comforting but bracing. Wise too. Maybe she made up every word he said, but it didn't feel like it. He often made her laugh. Although she loved Twig more than anyone else, she could not talk things over with him. He was too young and he knew so few words. Red Mouse was her faithful friend.

Get it over with. You're upsetting Twig, Red Mouse remarked.

Willow led the way back to the spot where they had first seen the kitten. There she let Twig wail in wordless pain while she scratched out a shallow grave in the bit of waste ground. One or two people passed by on the sidewalk but they did not even glance at the children, let alone ask what they were up to.

Willow grabbed a torn poster which was down in the gutter and used it to wrap the tiny body. Twig's sobs quieted as she laid the minute bundle in the hole and covered it over. He picked up a loose stone and laid it on the spot as though he knew a grave should be marked.

"Good boy, Twig," she said clearly.

Then she rose and took his hand. They walked and walked, side by side. Willow did not know what to do, where to make for. They could have walked to Crab Park. It wasn't far and Twig liked playing on the swings. But it was raining and chilly and Willow did not feel she could change into a swing pusher today. She did not want to go back to Maisie's either, but when darkness fell and the light drizzle turned to sleet, they had nowhere else to go.

She'll be worried, Red Mouse said. You owe her.

He was right. As they stumbled down the hall, Maisie herself peered out. She didn't smile or say a word but Willow knew she was relieved to see them safe and sound. She stood back to let them in and then, without speaking, served up supper. They were drooping with fatigue but they were hungry too and the food smelled good.

"Eat," Maisie said.

She had been to the Food Bank and they had Kraft Dinner. They had had Kraft Dinner for supper three days running and crackers and powdered milk for breakfast all week. Without margarine and real milk, Kraft Dinner was not great. But Willow and Twig were used to that. They cleaned their plates better than the best dishwasher could have done.

Twig took his last bite, put his head down on the table and fell instantly asleep. Willow hoisted him onto his feet, walked him to his sleeping bag and arranged him in it without his really waking up. Then she fetched water from the bathroom down the hall and rinsed the dishes. Replacing them on their shelf, she took a chair over to where Maisie sat slumped in front of her small black-and-white TV. Then she just sat, gathering her courage.

She won't bite you, Red Mouse said.

"Do you think Angel will come for us soon?" Willow asked, struggling not to let her voice shake.

Maisie showed no sign of having heard at first. Finally she turned to look at Willow. Her eyes held weariness and pity.

"She told me she was leaving you here for the weekend," she said. "It's been three months. She sent some money once but, apart from that, I haven't heard from her. There was no address with the cash."

"Oh," Willow said. "I thought she'd come by now."

"Last week, I ran into Rae. He says things got too hot for her and she split. He thinks she maybe went to Calgary."

Willow sat as still as a carved totem. She had guessed Angel would take her time about returning for them. She had not dreamed she would leave the city without moving the two of them somewhere else. Anybody with sense could see that neither Maisie's one room nor her meagre welfare cheque was large enough to house and feed three people.

Her mother said she loved them and Willow believed her. Angel could have had abortions or given them up to be adopted the way she herself had been. But she had kept them. That showed she cared about them in her own way. Even so, whenever she left them with someone, she let herself forget about them until something went wrong. Then she had to be tracked down and told to take care of her kids. Tracking her down was no cinch, though. It would be impossible if she'd left Vancouver.

Even Red Mouse was silent.

Willow stood up, walked up and down for a few seconds and then sat down again. She had to sit. Her legs felt like cheese strings.

"She's on parole. She's not supposed to leave Vancouver," she muttered.

"Yeah," Maisie grunted without taking her eyes off the foggy picture tube.

Angel had been in a brawl after the children had been brought back from Jo and Lou's. She had taken them with her to a wild party and, at midnight, long after Twig had fallen asleep on the floor, somebody had decided that they should raid a nearby convenience store for junk food. When Willow had realized Angel meant to go along, she had tried to talk her out of it but her mother had pushed her aside.

"You're my baby, not my mother, honey," she had said, her voice slurring with what she had had to drink on top of the drugs she took.

The party had been at Suzanne's place. Maisie had been there and she and Suzanne had agreed to watch the children while the rest were gone. Nobody had money to spend or, if anyone did, she was holding onto it.

Willow found out later that a teenage boy had been minding the store by himself that night. When he had refused to hand over what they wanted without being paid, they had trashed the place, breaking glass bottles, dumping out detergent, bleach and juice and dry cereal, throwing canned tomatoes at the walls. When the police arrived, they had all been taken into custody. Suzanne and Willow had grown more and more worried as hours passed without their showing up. Then Angel had telephoned and Suzanne had arranged to go collect them in the morning.

When the case was heard, Angel herself got off lightly. She had not been armed and she told the judge all about her babies who needed her. When she was sober and fully conscious, Angel could talk anybody around. Nevertheless, she had been put on parole and was forbidden to leave Vancouver. Her case was referred to Family Services. She had gone in for some sort of interview, but they had somehow missed the fact that Willow had never yet gone to school. They had all stayed at Suzanne's for a while, until she had had enough of

Twig's tantrums. Then Angel had talked Maisie into letting the children stay with her for a weekend.

Willow sighed. She felt as old as Maisie.

"Too bad you don't have other family," Maisie muttered. "What you need is kinfolks."

Willow glanced at her and looked away quickly, afraid the woman would see the picture that had sprung up in her mind. Gram. Gram's face, which she had not let herself glimpse for months, smiled at her as vividly and lovingly as ever.

Had Gram been the one who gave butterfly kisses? Willow rummaged in her mind, trying to fit scraps of memory together. Yes. Suddenly she was certain that Gram had been the one. Gram had taught her to read and sung her lullabies too. Willow could still sing two of them, although she knew there had been more. She had sung them to Twig in the first years of his life, when lullabies mattered to him.

Gram had sometimes roared at her, too, but Willow had not minded very much. You knew you were safe with Gram.

But I wasn't, Willow thought, desolation thrusting away her warm memories.

If only Gram had gone on wanting her, she would have someone to turn to now.

But Angel had been definite about that. Gram had told her not to bring Willow back. Ever! And now, even if she could be persuaded to accept Willow, it would not be enough. She would have to want Twig too. And Twig was hard for even his sister to handle. No old lady could be expected to cope with him.

Willow struggled to think of something else.

But the only picture that came was that of the dead kitten. Nobody had wanted it either.

Willow got up without a sound and went down the hall to the toilet. She didn't really have to go but it was better than brooding about the cat. On her way back she thought about her grandmother again. What if Angel had lied when she said, over and over, that Willow could not visit or even phone Gram because Gram herself had forbidden it?

"Your precious Gram said, 'She's your child and it's up to you to take care of her. Don't come running back here, when you get tired of playing mother.'"

Gram had also said it would be terrible for Willow to be bounced back and forth between her mother and grandmother as though she were nothing but a ping-pong ball.

"'If you take her now, you keep her,'" Angel's voice, bitter and angry, quoted once again inside Willow's head.

Might the stinging words have sounded different coming from her grandmother than they had when Angel repeated them? She might even have twisted them, added to them. Willow had heard her do that often. Things she herself had said, when quoted by her mother, had sounded funnier or more spiteful.

"I never said that," Willow had tried protesting.

"Of course you did. I was there, remember?" Angel would contradict.

And whoever was being told the story always believed Angel's version.

Angel had told lots of other out-and-out lies, too, over the years. She said she'd be back and she never came. She said Julius was going to marry her and he didn't. She even made Willow lie.

"Tell them you're my little sister," she had said more than once. "I'm too young to have a kid your size."

The thought that Gram might have only said those things to keep Angel from taking her away cheered Willow up for a few seconds. Yet, if that were the truth, why had her grandmother never tried to make contact with them? Because of her grandmother's parting words, Twig and Willow had ended up being treated like a couple of parcels dumped in a locker at the bus station and forgotten. She had turned them into nobody's children.

Don't forget the butterfly kisses, Red Mouse put in.

If only I knew where to find Gram, she thought.

Staring at her worn sneakers, Willow felt rage growing inside her, fury against Angel and Julius, Jo and Lou, Maisie and all the other "friends" whom Angel had dumped them with over the years. She could see them, faces flickering in and out, smiling, pitying, but not there to be turned to now for help. There had been Lisette and Jackie, Zoe, who said her name meant "Life," Suzanne . . . Angel had had men friends too. "He's a good guy, Willow," she had said about a couple of them. Danny had taken them out for dinner at White Spot several times. Tony had given them presents, big stuffed bears and Barbies. Angel had taken the toys and sold them later, except for the Pocahontas doll: she had been left behind at Jo and Lou's. Willow had not had time for dolls after Twig came. Yes, Angel had other friends but they were not the kind of people to look after Willow and Twig if something happened to Maisie.

Yet Gram, who was that kind, had not rescued them, not even tried. Butterfly kisses were not enough.

"Don't let it get you down, kid," Maisie broke in on Willow's tumbling thoughts. "I just thought Angel must have had people. She can read books, you know, so she has more schooling than most of us down here. She didn't hit the streets until she was seventeen or eighteen. Someone looked after her until then. Still, I don't have any relatives I care to own, so why should she?"

"Right," Willow mumbled.

"Angel left some stuff for me to take care of for her. You should have it in case something happens to me. I don't feel so good lately."

"Nothing's going to happen to you," Willow cried, fighting down panic.

"No, but you take her papers all the same," Maisie said, shuffling over to her sagging bed. "You pull that box out for me."

Willow hauled out the cardboard box Maisie indicated. The old woman, wheezing almost as badly as the dying kitten had done, sat down on the bed and digging through a mass of stuff, produced a brown envelope, torn at one corner. "Here you are. Now let's hit the sack."

Willow stuffed the envelope into her sleeping bag. Then she turned to face the old woman who was easing off her slippers.

"I can't . . . I don't know when Angel . . . " she began and stopped.

She longed to promise that she and her brother would be picked up first thing in the morning but she knew there was really no chance.

"I don't know either," muttered Maisie. "We're not much

good to each other, are we, honey? Don't worry. I won't turn you out. She's bound to show up soon."

Willow swallowed, tried to speak and couldn't. Maisie rose creakily and switched off the blurry, jiggling people on the TV screen. She went back to her bed, sat down and waited to catch her breath. She let a full minute pass before she said, "We'll have to think of something, child. Rae was too interested in you. I doubt I'll be alive much longer. If you aren't out of here by then, he'll turn you into a junkie in short order. You'll end up like your mother. Angel has her good points. She's helped me out more than once when she had money and I was flat broke. But she hasn't got your common sense or your strength. Maybe it comes from looking after that boy. It's been rough but it's made you tough."

She paused and stared at Willow as though she were measuring her toughness. Then she went on, her voice lower, slurred with tiredness.

"I didn't like Rae's asking about the two of you. Rae gave Angel her first fix. 'A pick-me-up,' he told her. She thought she could quit any time until she tried. I've known Rae since he was a kid and I can tell you that he's bad news."

Willow stared at her, fear stiffening her face. Maisie, catching it, stopped short. But she had said enough. Rae was a frequent visitor to Maisie's building. Angel was afraid of him and had warned Willow to keep out of his sight. She did not need Maisie to tell her Rae was bad news.

"Time for bed. Things may look better in the morning," Maisie said as she heaved herself up and headed out the door to the bathroom, which was shared by everyone on the floor.

Taking off only her shoes, Willow slid herself back into

her sleeping bag without bothering to wrestle with the broken zipper. She held her mother's envelope against her chest and wanted to open it. But she was so tired and she didn't want Maisie to watch her while she looked. Whatever Angel had saved could wait until morning.

She wrenched her mind away from thoughts of her mother and Gram because, if she did not, she might begin to cry. She hardly ever cried, never when anyone might see. Crying let people know you hurt. Once they did that, they pitied you. Willow Wind Jones despised pity and she was not about to take it, even from Maisie.

She pushed the envelope deep down to the foot of the bag and curled up on one side, but she could not sleep. She lay wracking her brain for somewhere she could go if worse came to worst, somebody she could ask for help. Red Mouse, small, velvet-soft and visible only to herself, was a comfort but he could not feed Twig and her. If she couldn't call her grandmother, the only place she could think of was the police station.

She shrank from the very idea. Nobody she knew trusted the police.

"Scum," Angel called them.

Well, she would just have to wait for Angel, she decided finally. She had no other choice. Now she must sleep. She called up her picture of Red Mouse as a baby with Mammy Mouse. They always helped her grow drowsy. She did not know where he had come from but, whenever she needed to escape from the difficulties of her life with Twig, Red Mouse was waiting.

He looked like any other mouse except he was scarlet and

especially velvety. Adults never saw him. Cats never saw him either. He could talk and he could fly and he could fit inside her pocket. When Mammy Mouse put him to bed, she always sang the same lullaby. Willow, humming it softly so Maisie would not hear, felt small and cosy and comforted.

> Pull in your tail, Red Mouse, Red Mouse.
> Pull in your tail, Red Mousie.
> For the best little mouse is a little red mouse
> Who is falling asleep in his Red Mouse House.

By the time Red Mouse had pulled in his whiskers, his paws and his round, red ears, Willow was asleep.

Then, the next afternoon, before Willow had found enough private minutes to investigate what lay inside Angel's envelope, Maisie collapsed.

2
Willow's Darkest Hour

Willow saw it happen. On Wednesday morning, Maisie had gone out to pick up her welfare cheque. Knowing she should be back, Willow went to meet her and help her up the stairs. She saw the old woman come shuffling back into the building. Then, just as Willow started to run down to her, Maisie staggered, dropped her purse, reached out for the wall and crumpled up in a heap on the floor.

Willow began to race down to her when Rae, who was on his way out, came across them. He hunkered down next to Maisie, searched her shabby purse with lightning speed and rose, her cheque in his hand. Willow, frozen with shock, watched him stow the envelope away and then pull out his cellular phone. He called for an ambulance, giving a fake name but the right address.

"Move it or the old dame'll be dead before you get here,"

he said. His flat voice and harsh words implied Maisie was a complete stranger to him. Willow knew better.

"He was a sweet child before his mum took off and his dad started knocking him about," Maisie had said once, after Rae had paused to greet her in the hall. "Now he's nothing but trouble."

"How old . . . ?" Willow had begun to ask.

"I know you think I'm as old as Methuselah," Maisie had answered the unfinished question. "But I'm not quite sixty, Miss Willow Jones. I knew Rae's mother. I saw him the day he was born. I was a ward aide then at the hospital."

Willow could not hide her surprise. Maisie looked older than the mountains. She was bent and gaunt.

"If I had teeth, I wouldn't look like such a crone," she had said.

"You do have some teeth," Willow had said, hesitating over the words.

"I do. Six of them. Praise the Lord they can still chew," Maisie had laughed. "They'll last me till I'm done with this world."

Alert suddenly to her own danger, the girl on the stairs began to back silently out of the man's sight, but he glanced up.

"Hold it, kid," he called, his voice hard as granite.

The ten-year-old froze. She kept her chin up but, despite herself, her lips curved into a nervous smile meant to disarm him. He looked her over slowly from her shaggy black head to her sneakers.

Then his taxi, which had been idling at the corner, pulled to the curb and honked. Rae and his girlfriend always travelled in cabs. Through the open door to the street, Willow could just glimpse her slouched in the back seat, her red hair falling over her face. Judging from her lolling position, she was probably already stoned.

Rae glared at the driver but started to leave.

"Stick around, kid. I'll be back. I'll take care of you. I'll take care of the boy too. If anybody tries to muscle in, tell them Rae's coming for you," he called over his shoulder.

· Willow watched the taxi drive away. When she was certain it was gone, she shivered. She and Twig would have to disappear before he came back. Because Rae meant what he said, and Rae was poison.

Automatically, she started down again, to check on Maisie, and then halted. She mustn't be caught here by whoever Rae had phoned. She could tell from where she stood that, if Maisie was not dead yet, she was close to it. She had not moved since she fell and Willow, straining her ears, could not hear her breathing. Maisie's breath always wheezed a bit. If Willow were caught by the paramedics, they'd ask questions and later report her presence to someone with authority. If they failed to do so, Rae would come for her as he had said he would.

Red Mouse spoke sharply. Get Twig and leave now! Move!

Willow raced back to Maisie's room where her little brother sat mesmerized by Woody Woodpecker on the TV. Without interrupting him, Willow got the box of soda crackers out. There were only four left. She ate one and made Twig eat the rest. He was so much easier to handle when he was not hungry. Then she sat in Maisie's chair and forced herself to think.

No grand inspiration came. She could not afford to wait for one. She listened for the siren of the ambulance. The shrill cry of it cut off abruptly. She was tense, ready to spring into action if she heard them coming up the stairs. Twig eyed her uneasily but went on munching his last cracker. The siren started up again.

Willow jumped up. She fished Angel's envelope out from the bottom of her sleeping bag and shoved it into her ragged backpack. Then she took Twig firmly by the hand and led him out the door. He looked up at her with a frown but he came, leaving behind the only security they knew.

They went down the stairs and out the door and began walking. Without Willow's planning it, they ended up at Crab Park. Twig ran straight to the playground equipment, wriggled up onto a swing and yelled at her to give him a push.

The moment she was within sight of the little park, Willow's fear let go its stranglehold on her. Her hammering heart slowed down a fraction. Crab Park and the much larger Stanley Park were two places she loved. When she was five, she had come here with her mother. When she was older, six maybe, Angel and Julius had taken her to Stanley Park for a picnic just before Angel told him she was expecting a baby and Julius walked out.

Willow pushed Twig's swing and remembered going into the Aquarium with Julius. How she had loved it! She had stood as close as she could get to the whales and imagined herself sliding through the water effortlessly.

"Poor things!" Angel had said.

"Why are they poor?" Willow had asked, never taking her eyes off the huge gliding shapes.

"They should be swimming free in the ocean instead of being captives here," said her mother.

Yet, to Willow, they had seemed miraculously free. They were never hungry or hunted to feed others. They were not awkward or slow. They felt no fear. They were safe in their tanks. And they were so beautiful.

A laughing Angel finally had to drag Willow away.

Three months ago, a couple of days before she left them with Maisie, Angel had taken them both to Stanley Park. She had not had enough money that time to get into the Aquarium but Twig had been enchanted by the polar bears. It was their last happy afternoon together.

Those months with Julius, before her mother was pregnant with Twig, held some of Willow's best memories. Julius had made Angel laugh so much. Happy-go-lucky. That was the word for him.

Twig began to kick his feet hard. He had had enough of swinging. She slowed the swing until he could jump off. Then, wandering through the park with him holding her hand, Willow felt desperate. A great lump came into her throat as she found herself yearning for Julius.

Yet he would not come even if he knew how she needed him. She could still hear his voice saying so lightly, "Hey, Angel, I can't handle being Daddy. I like your Willow but I don't want any baby calling me Dad and that's final."

Angel had had an abortion that time but, with Twig, she had not figured out she was pregnant until it was too late. When she broke the news, Julius had listened to her talk and cry and promise the baby would be no trouble. Then he had gone out to rent a video and pick up some beer.

"See you," he had called back from the doorway.

But, although they waited up until after midnight, he had

not come back. Angel had searched for him the next day and, on being told he had left Vancouver on the first bus, she had gone back to the drugs for comfort and escape.

"If Julius had just waited to meet you . . . " Willow said to Twig.

But it would have made no difference. Because Angel had been on drugs throughout the pregnancy, Twig had been born addicted. Willow knew, with absolute certainty, that happy-go-lucky Julius could not have endured Twig's screaming and his anguished body arching as he suffered through withdrawal.

Then Willow caught a glimpse of Lion's Gate Bridge. She stood absolutely still and smiled her first real smile in hours. Like the Aquarium, Lion's Gate Bridge made her feel joyous, strong, lifted up high as the sky. It was so lofty, so immense, so powerful. Yet Willow Wind Jones could walk across it. If only she and Twig could go there now and stand looking out over English Bay and think about sailing far away on one of the ships they saw!

But the bridge, although it looked near, was too far. Twig was too small. And she had to think where they were to sleep tonight.

She pulled her little brother to a secluded bench. Rae would not look for them here. She could take time to plan.

"Hey there, chick," a thick voice said.

Before the leering man knew what was happening, Willow was up and away, hauling a stumbling, furious Twig after her. She wished she could make him understand. But she knew it was no use trying.

"It'll have to be the police," she muttered. "They won't

beat up kids. They might know where Angel's gotten herself."

Don't hold your breath, Red Mouse murmured.

Willow ignored him and began walking again. She dragged Twig along, striding too quickly, forgetting he had no idea what was happening. Then she saw a police station across the street and halted.

She could not go there. She could not . . .

"Wo," Twig whimpered at last. "Wo!"

His sister leaned down to face him, put her finger to his lips and shook her head at him. He reared back, twisting his head away. Then, seeing she was not angry, he leaned against her. His bottom lip jutted out ominously. If she did not find a place where he could rest, he was going to throw one of his tantrums. It was time to cross the street and ask for help.

Yet Willow delayed a few seconds longer, staring over at the uninviting building. Until she and Twig went through those doors, she was in charge and the two of them were independent.

"Sure. Independently starving. Independently homeless too," she jeered at herself.

She yanked Twig through a break in the traffic. He yelped but came stumbling after her.

The two of them shot across the busy street. A man in a truck just missed hitting Willow and she heard him swear at her as she leaped to safety. Then they were going into the police station itself. Willow took one terrified glance around and ducked her head so that her shaggy bangs curtained her face. Twig, confused, let his sister tug him into the corner of the room farthest from the desk. Willow sat down abruptly on the couch near the elevator and pulled him into the space between herself and the wall. Then she stayed absolutely still, waiting for her heart to stop thudding against her ribs and her breathing to steady before she made her next move. It was not going to be easy.

Count backwards from fifty, Red Mouse advised.

Willow ignored him, but knowing he was with her helped her to grow calmer. Then she glanced around the large, unfriendly space. Angel would never have come here for help.

You had no other choice, Red Mouse reminded her.

It was true. She might have made it on her own, tracked down her mother even, but she had her brother to think about. Comforting as Red Mouse was, he could not find them food to eat or a safe place to sleep. She, Willow Wind Jones, would have to ask the cops for help and be grateful for whatever she got.

Waiting was agonizing. Twig stared wide-eyed at the strangers clustered around the desk. His sister, seeing his bewilderment, sighed. Even if she could explain to him what was going on, a four-year-old could not help much. As usual, it was up to her.

"Wo . . . " he began.

She put her finger to his lips again before anyone noticed his strange, extra-loud voice. Faking calm, she gazed into his puzzled eyes, smiled and shook her head again. This time, although he got the message, he was fed up. He pushed away from her, leaving a space between them. She braced herself for what he would do next.

Miraculously, he yawned and slumped against her again.

His eyes grew unfocused. She watched him will himself into a sleep so deep he might have been drugged.

Willow had grown worried recently about these sleeps of Twig's but she was thankful now. If only he would go on sleeping until she had a chance to ask somebody where she could find her mother and ask her what they should do. If only the people would listen! Adults, especially policemen, were all bad at listening when the person talking was a "dirty little Indian brat."

She was dirty. Maisie had no running water. And the water she fetched from the washroom at the end of the hall was always ice-cold. Not good for washing in.

Willow swallowed hard and shifted restlessly. The big envelope in her backpack rustled. Now was as good a time as any. She pulled it out and undid the string holding it shut. Putting her hand in, she slowly drew out a surprising catch.

On top was a paperback picture book. Willow stared at it with uncomprehending eyes. Why would Angel keep this? She opened it to the first page and read.

> *Mammy Mouse's new baby was not like the other seven. Scoot and Scout and Scurry and Scamper and Skip and Skeezix and Skedaddle were pink and hairless when they were born. Their eyes were shut and they had no ears to speak of.*
> *But the new baby had wide-open eyes, perky stand-up ears and he was not pink.*
> *He was red.*

Willow turned the page, unable to believe her eyes.

> *He was as red as a tomato.*
> *He was as red as a cardinal.*
> *He was as red as a scarlet geranium.*
> *And his skin was velvety like a geranium petal.*

She turned another page and read on.

> *Mammy Mouse stared at him.*
> *"What can you name a red mouse?" she cried.*
> *"How about Red Mouse?" said Pappy Mouse.*

Willow flipped back to the cover and read the title. Red Mouse Plays a Trick, by Humphrey Gordon. She stared at the author's name and tried to make sense of it. Who was this person who had put Red Mouse in a book? He was her Red Mouse. She even knew the names of his seven sisters. She turned to the back cover and saw a paragraph about the author.

> *Humphrey Gordon, prize-winning author of eighteen*
> *children's books, has now written his first picture book.*
> *Mr. Gordon, blind since the age of twelve, lives in a*
> *farmhouse in southwestern Ontario, with his sister Nell*
> *and his Seeing Eye dog Sirius. Mr. Gordon was inspired*
> *to write about Red Mouse by his great-niece, to whom*
> *the book is dedicated.*

There was no picture of him. Willow's hands started

shaking. She closed the book and shoved it back into the envelope, ripping it slightly in her rush. The bit about Humphrey Gordon bewildered her. But the picture of Red Mouse made her furious. The illustrator had made him cute, cartoonish, with a too sharp nose and huge ears. Red Mouse did not look anything like that. He was real and caring and . . .

You are absolutely right, came his voice. I am no smirking, show-off, poor excuse for a rodent. I am the essence of mouse and I am yours.

"Yes," Willow whispered. She glanced at the assortment of folded papers but could not bear to look at anything else while she sat trapped in the waiting room of a police station. The other papers would have to wait until she was alone. She felt dizzy with shock as it was.

If only the woman at the desk would hurry up and notice them and realize that they were on their own!

There was a big clock on the wall. Fifteen minutes crawled past. It felt like at least an hour. Willow's stomach rumbled.

Then a young policeman, who looked Chinese, stopped by their corner.

"Are you with somebody?" he asked.

Willow glared at the floor and shook her head. The woman behind the desk spoke sharply, giving the young man the kind of look people often directed at Twig.

"I've been watching those two, Constable. I saw them come in. I've already called Family Services. Abandoned kids are their business. You're not on duty, are you?"

"No, but they're just—"

"We're not a clearing house for homeless brats," she snapped. "This is a police station, not a day-care centre."

A middle-aged couple hurried up to the desk and, both shouting at once, began telling of waking up to find their car stolen. The nasty desk sergeant forgot Willow and Twig for the moment. The nice young constable's smile did not waver.

"Would you like a Coke and something to eat while you wait?" he asked softly. "I'm going out for doughnuts and coffee."

Without stopping to think, Willow Jones shook her head again. Twig was still sleeping. One thing was for sure. Nobody was waking Twig to ask him if he wanted food, not if Willow had anything to say about it. Twig asleep might be a tremendous worry to her, Twig awake would be hell on wheels.

Take it, Red Mouse commanded. You need sustenance.

"Are you sure? You look hungry to me," the man said, his tone friendly. He was giving her another chance.

Willow darted a suspicious glance up at him. His black eyes were kind. Maybe he was too young to have turned mean. And maybe hunger was part of Twig's problem. Then Willow realized, all at once, that she herself was famished. They had not eaten a bite since they finished Maisie's box of soda crackers. No wonder her stomach was growling. Red Mouse was right as usual.

"We can't pay," she muttered.

"My treat. What'll it be?"

"Chips?" she half-whispered, not looking at him.

"Chips it is," he said. "I'll be back in two shakes. Keep your chin up, kid. The darkest hour comes just before the dawn."

The big door swung shut behind him. Willow could hear

him whistling as he strode away down the hall. She recognized the tune. It was one Angel had often sung.

> *Like a bridge over troubled water*
> *I will lay me down . . .*

Angel had sung the words, but she had never been a trustworthy bridge when her children needed one. Sitting on the hard bench in the police station with her small brother asleep beside her, Willow Jones felt that she, dragging Twig along, was forever battling through deep, dangerous rivers while up above, other people, Angel among them, waltzed over high and dry on nice, safe bridges. Hardly anyone looked down and noticed them. The lucky ones never stopped to stretch out a helping hand.

Except for that cop. What had he said? Trying not to think about food, she concentrated on his words.

"The darkest hour comes just before the dawn."

That was it. She wished it were true. If dawn was coming, Willow could not see any sign of it.

3
A Call for Help

It was then that Willow first noticed herself and Twig reflected in the darkened glass of a large window opposite their bench. Trying to take her mind off Maisie and Rae, Angel and even Red Mouse, who might not be her secret alone, she studied the picture she and her sleeping brother made.

Even though they had the same mother, they did not resemble each other at first glance. She looked 100-percent native. She was too thin and her grubby clothes were all a bit too big or too small. Her hair, dulled by dirt, was jet black and poker straight. Her shaggy bangs were too long and cut decidedly crooked. She chopped them off herself whenever they started interfering with her vision, and she didn't care how they looked. Her eyebrows were thick for a ten-year-old. Her bright black eyes stared somberly back at her from under them. Her nose was snub and her mouth turned down at the corners. The set of her chin showed she'd fight if she had to. She'd proved that more than once. She was not pretty but she liked her face just fine.

Twig, curled up next to her, looked as though he belonged to some other family. Well, Julius, his father, had come from Jamaica or Trinidad.

"The Islands," Angel had said.

Willow gazed at Twig's reflection and almost smiled. He had short, springy, black curls and skin the colour of coffee with lots of cream in it. Behind his closed eyelids, he had big, velvety brown eyes. His grin was impish and, even when he was serious, he had an appealing look. Maybe the two deep dimples in his cheeks had something to do with it. Although he was fatter than she was, he was too thin. They had had slim pickings with Maisie. But his dimples still showed.

"Winsome Twig," Lou had called him.

"With eyes like pansies," Jo had said.

If only he didn't get so wild! When he was screaming and kicking, nobody saw his winsome side. Sometimes his rages were so terrible that he scared even Willow, who loved him with her whole being. The outbursts went on and on and became incredibly loud. People who didn't know him at all thought he was crazy. She had heard them muttering this to one another. If anyone ever said it directly to her, she planned to punch them out.

Willow shifted slightly and glowered at the policewoman, who was not only ignoring them but was now being rude to the couple whose car had gone missing. Willow wanted to get it over with. She really needed to go to the bathroom, for one thing. And the longer she sat here, the lonelier and more tight with tension she felt.

Two bags of potato chips dropped into her lap, close to Twig's unconscious head. Willow looked up.

"I got you juice," the Chinese cop said. "You can take your pick. Orange or apple?"

"Orange," Willow muttered. Her lips curved up a little in spite of her. Maybe he saw. He opened the orange juice and handed it to her complete with a straw.

Willow sucked up the juice greedily. Then she ripped open one bag of chips and began to eat, forcing herself to take them out one by one instead of stuffing in whole fist-fuls. Who knew when she'd eat next? She had to make them last.

The friendly cop was standing nearby, sipping his coffee out of a disposable cup. Not knowing what to say to him, she pretended not to notice his glancing over at her. The chips tasted heavenly. She could have eaten all of hers and Twig's too. When she finished, and, licking the last bit of salty vine-gar off her fingers, left Twig's bag unopened, the man reached into a big paper sack he was carrying and handed her a fat honey-glazed doughnut.

"Here's dessert," he said quietly.

"Thanks," she growled, glaring at the floor as though it had insulted her. She knew she should smile up at him but she couldn't, not without bursting into tears. No cop, how-ever kind, was going to see Angel Jones's kid cry.

Willow gobbled the doughnut down and felt stronger. First the chips and juice and then the doughnut, plus the unexpected generosity of one man, had warmed the cold

31

emptiness and tumbling confusion inside her so that she felt she might be able to face what came next.

"Well, back to the treadmill," the cop said, tossing his coffee cup into a litter bin in the corner.

Willow opened her mouth and then closed it. All her life she had been told the cops were her enemies. One had roughed up her mother when she was pregnant with Twig. But this man was not like that. She might even be able to talk to him. She shot a glance at his face.

"Did you want to ask me something, kiddo?" he said.

She wanted to ask him what he meant about the darkest hour but she didn't. There were other things she needed to know first.

"What's going to happen to us?" She spoke so softly that most people would have made her repeat herself. But he heard her.

"I don't know," he said. "Who brought you . . . ?"

"Thank you, Constable Chang," the woman's sharp voice broke in again. "I'll ask the questions, if you don't mind. They're next."

She came out from behind the desk and pulled a chair up in front of the bench where the children sat. She wrinkled up her nose then and backed up a bit. The man gave Willow an apologetic smile, waved and left the front office. Willow understood that he had no choice, but she felt abandoned all the same.

"I'm Sergeant Evans," the woman said, her tone coolly businesslike. "I've called Family Services. They're sending someone over so you needn't worry. I was going to wait for her but . . . "

Willow, peering out from under her ragged bangs, took in the trim neatness of the policewoman. This smooth-talking, cold-eyed being had never once in her life not known where she'd eat and sleep for weeks to come. She'd had plenty of hot water too, and sweet-smelling soap and always clean clothes to put on. She'd be shocked out of her skull by Maisie's place. It wasn't Willow's fault if they smelled a bit.

"I'll save time by getting some answers. What is your name?"

Why did they always start with that? Willow, not for the first time, considered lying. But her strange name was one of the two things that belonged to her. Her name and her brother.

"Willow," she muttered.

"Wilma?"

"No. Willow."

"Willa?"

"Not Willa. Willow."

"Willow? You mean, like the willow tree?"

"That's it. Willow."

"Is that all? Have you a surname?"

"Of course," Willow said, trying to hide her uncertainty behind a defiant mask. "My whole name is Willow Wind Jones."

"My Lord, what'll they think of next?" the woman said, writing the name down with distaste. "And the boy? Is his name Jones too?"

Willow stiffened. She was not 100-percent sure about Twig's legal surname. But they must share a last name or somebody would be sure to think of separating them.

"He's Twig."

"Are you kidding me?"

"No," Willow said stonily. "Everyone calls him Twig. Twig Jones."

She knew that Twig's real first name might have to come out eventually but she was not telling unless she had no other choice.

"Who sent you here?"

Willow's head jerked up as the question slammed into her.

"Nobody," she said, keeping an iron grip on her self-control. "We had nowhere else to go. If we did, we wouldn't be here."

"Where did you sleep last night? Tell the truth, mind."

"In the park," Willow lied. She was not dragging Maisie into it. They weren't Maisie's kids, they were Angel's.

"What park?"

The woman's contempt made Willow's cheeks grow hot. She was glad her dark skin almost hid the flush. She dropped her head and answered dully. "I don't know its name." She tried to leave it there but the outrage she felt made her tack on, "What does its name matter?"

"Don't use that tone of voice when you speak to me," Sergeant Evans snapped, her eyes hard as bullets. "Somebody put you up to this."

She went on staring at Willow for a moment but Willow's will was a match for hers. Finally, her glance slid over to Twig, still asleep and now sucking his very dirty thumb.

"What about your parents?"

Willow made her face as blank as the wall behind her.

"I never knew my father," she said in a low voice. "My

mother left us with a friend who took off yesterday. I don't know where she went."

That's good, kid, Red Mouse encouraged her. You're three steps ahead of her all the way.

Willow almost smiled but stopped herself before Sergeant Evans saw. The policewoman snorted and capped her pen.

"They'll find you a good foster home," she said, staring at Willow as though she were a hardened criminal. "Maybe the little one will even be adopted. Some people are so desperate they'll risk taking a child his size. You certainly aren't a fit person to be looking after him."

Willow, weary and worried, had grown momentarily dazed. The word "adopted" shocked her back into wide-awake attention. The fear of being parted from Twig made her think of the envelope Maisie had given her. Wasn't there an address on one of the pages?

The phone rang and Sergeant Evans, swearing under her breath, went to get it. Willow breathed a prayer of thanks-giving to Red Mouse or her guardian angel or whoever it was that was helping her. She pulled out the handful of folded papers and grubby business envelopes. Several were clearly letters from Nell Jones. Gram had written!

Willow did not allow herself to think about it, not yet. There were address labels stuck on the envelopes. When Sergeant Evans came back, Willow was ready.

"I . . . We do have other family," she blurted, before the woman was properly seated. "Here's my grandmother's address. Her name's Mrs. Jones. I'm sure she'll want us both to come and live with her. We can get her phone number from the operator, can't we?"

35

She ran out of breath then and stopped. The police-woman took the envelope Willow held out. She stared at it with distaste, holding it gingerly, as though it might bite. Even after examining it, she still appeared skeptical.

"We'll try Directory Assistance," she said in a dry voice. "She may have moved on from this address."

"No," Willow said firmly. "She'll still be there."

She had no idea why she was so sure. In her memories, Gram was not someone who moved from place to place. She was a stayer.

"Hmm. Is she native?"

Willow pretended not to hear. It didn't matter. Also, she was not absolutely sure of the right answer. In her mental picture, Gram's face was bronzed as though she spent a lot of time in the sun. All she knew for certain was that, somewhere deep in the past, a beloved voice had sung,

> *Hush, little Willow, don't say a word,*
> *Grammy's going to buy you a mockingbird.*

There were the butterfly kisses, too, and other memories. She had pushed them away for so long that she couldn't find them without taking time to think her way back. Once upon a time, she thought she had clung to them but, when Twig was hurt and nobody came to rescue them, she had made herself stop remembering.

"Her brother is a writer," she said, searching the scraps of memory she could bring up. "My mum said so."

"What's his name?"

"I can't remember," Willow muttered.

Was he the man who had written the book about Red Mouse? She had no idea. She did not remember the book arriving. She was almost positive she had never laid eyes on it before today. Why had Angel kept it from her? Perhaps it had come during the time she had spent with Jo and Lou. Angel would have forgotten about it before she next saw them.

"How old is this grandmother? Is she married? Oh, here's Ms Thornton. These are the children I called about. They turned up here a couple of hours ago, claiming they've got no family but a grandmother in Ontario and no place to go. We can probably hunt down their mother though, given time . . . "

Ms Thornton pulled up another chair and smiled at Willow. Willow watched her eyes to see if the smile was real. It was. Tired and discouraged, maybe, but kind. Like the young policeman. Her eyes were the colour of the ocean on a sunny day.

Willow was aching with fatigue but she did her best to keep her wits about her. She picked up the envelopes the woman had dropped and held them out again. She explained once more the little she knew about Gram.

"Wonderful," Ms Thornton said, her face brightening visibly. "We'll call her."

Gratitude flooded through Willow. It was such a relief to have an adult not only listen to her and believe what she said but treat her as though what she had to say mattered.

"Wait," she told them. She turned to her brother and shook him gently. When Twig's eyes opened, she put the potato chips into his hand and unscrewed the lid of the juice bottle.

"You eat," she told him. "I'm going to talk to our Gram. I'll be right over there."

As Twig began to stuff in the chips, Willow ran to the desk where the telephone sat.

"Let me talk to her," she said. "If you get the number to ring, let me talk first."

She was not sure why this mattered. But she knew it did. Sergeant Evans started to refuse but Ms Thornton said, "Of course you may.

"If there's any chance she'll take them," she explained to the policewoman, "we'll grab it. We're overloaded as it is. I can bed them down tonight if it's absolutely necessary, but . . . "

In Ontario, the phone began to ring. Sergeant Evans handed the receiver to Willow. She clutched it so tightly her hand ached.

The phone rang and rang with no answer. Willow thought she would burst into tears but she didn't. Twig had finished his chips and drained the juice bottle. He came over and huddled against his sister, looking ruffled up and sleepy like a baby owl.

"Hello," said a faraway voice finally, a voice she knew.

"This is Willow," Willow whispered.

"Pardon," said the voice. "I'm having trouble hearing."

"This is Willow," she said, fighting off a rush of tears. "I'm your daughter Angel's little girl. Twig is my brother. We have nowhere left to go. I found your address on an envelope . . . "

"Let me speak to her," the policewoman said, grabbing the receiver from Willow's fist. She explained and went on explaining.

"Would you like me to see about foster home placement?" she asked finally.

Gram made some answer. Willow tried to read it in the woman's cold face.

"Well, of course, I don't know anything about you," Sergeant Evans said, sounding mad as hops. "It's just . . . you should be told a few facts before you do anything rash. These children look as though they've been living on the street. The older one is definitely native and the little boy . . . he's clearly mentally handicapped. I can't tell what race . . . "

She broke off, flushed scarlet and almost spat her next words into the phone.

"I'm well aware they belong to the human race, madam. But they waltzed in here and claimed they're homeless. I'm responsible at the moment. I can't hand them over to just anybody without at least checking . . . I mean, are you young enough, Mrs. Jones, to handle two juveniles . . . "

They all heard Gram swear. Willow turned her face away so Sergeant Evans would not see her grin. Ms Thornton, she saw, was doing much the same.

"All right. I heard you. We'll send them. But we'll need references. We can't simply ship——"

Sergeant Evans's mouth clamped shut in a thin line. Then she took a breath and gave the receiver back to Willow.

"She wants to talk to you again," she said, her voice betraying outrage. Whatever her Gram had said must have rocked her.

Way to go, Gram, Willow thought.

"Hello. This is Willow," she said.

"This is your Gram. Do you remember your Uncle Star?

Well, it doesn't matter. He's living out there too. I'll call him and get him to put you on a plane and I'll be there to meet it," said the faraway warm voice. "You haven't been officially apprehended by the Children's Aid. I asked. And I am your legal grandmother. I can even get Angel's permission, if I have to. I know a way to get in touch with her. We can sort things out together."

Willow had to gulp down a giant lump in her throat before she could speak.

"Twig too?" she croaked at last.

She heard a sound which was half sigh, half rueful laugh.

"Twig too," said her grandmother. "Of course, Twig too."

4
Fly Away Home

Ms Thornton spoke to Gram next.

"Of course I won't apprehend the children if they have a good home to go to," she said. "I'm not searching for kids to put into foster care, believe me. If you can get their uncle over . . . yes, yes. Get him to bring proof of his identity . . . No, not if I don't apprehend them . . . His name's what? . . . Stardust!"

She burst out laughing.

"Sorry," she said, her eyes dancing. "I've just met a child called Willow with a brother called Twig and a mother called Angel. I should have guessed she'd have an Uncle Stardust. Of course, you couldn't change their names when they already knew themselves as Angel and Star. How old was Angel?"

She listened again, smiling.

"Fine. Call me back when you get him. The kids and I will wait to hear from you . . . "

She hung up. Sergeant Evans raised her thin eyebrows and said coolly, "It sounds fishy to me. Nervy too, as though this station is a recycling depot for unwanted brats. How do we know this woman is legit?"

"I'll take any flak," Ms Thornton said in a level voice. "I know their mother. After her arrest, I was supposed to apprehend the children but she persuaded me they were well cared for. It was very moving."

"She's good at talking," Willow said.

"Yes indeed," Ms Thornton said. "I shouldn't have been taken in but she had all of us wound around her little finger."

The other woman gave a disgusted snort.

"Trash like her shouldn't be allowed to have kids," she said.

Ms Thornton flashed one icy glance at her and then turned her body so that, although she still faced Willow, her back was toward the policewoman. Willow longed to kick Sergeant Evans in the shins but squeezed her rage down inside herself until it could be shoved into the inner place where she stored her furies. She then followed the caseworker's example and acted as though Sergeant Evans had never existed. She knew, from years of experience, how people hated it when she stopped noticing their presence. It was her way of controlling Twig when nothing else worked.

"Do you know where Angel is now?" she asked too softly for the police sergeant to hear.

Ms Thornton shook her head.

The phone shrilled. Sergeant Evans picked up the receiver. It was Gram asking to speak to Ms Thornton.

When the social worker hung up, she gave Willow a wide smile.

"Your Uncle Star will be here in half an hour," she said. "Your grandmother got the two of you on the Red Eye flight, leaving just after midnight. Your uncle will put you on the plane and you'll be met in Toronto by your grandmother. That lady doesn't waste time, does she? Wow! I wish she worked in our office."

Willow watched Red Mouse turn a neat cartwheel. Gram was coming to the rescue. Willow felt her whole body go limp with relief until, without any warning, Twig began to scream.

"What on earth . . . ?" Sergeant Evans shouted over the racket. She stared at the small, scarlet-faced boy as though he were an enemy alien. "That child sounds demented."

Willow sprang in front of her brother and gave the two women a look that cut like a switchblade. Why couldn't they see for themselves how frightened and tired he was? He was barely four, after all. She put one hand behind her on his rigid shoulder. Then she yelled the only thing she knew they would understand.

"He's hungry and he has to pee."

She could not go on. But Constable Chang appeared as if by magic. He swung Twig up into his arms.

"Follow me," he told Willow and strode away.

At the washroom door, he slid Twig to the floor and, reaching into his own pocket, handed Willow a black comb. She was so grateful she wanted to hug him. Instead she closed the door and unzipped Twig's ragged jeans.

"Listen to me, Twig," she said right into his ear. "Shut up, shut up, shut up! If you don't be quiet, I'll leave you."

She wouldn't, and both of them knew it. But it was the one threat that never failed. Without her, Twig would be

43

utterly lost. His eyes wide, his hot cheeks wet with tears, the little boy gulped, closed his mouth and started to pee.

Willow took a deep breath and backed off a step. Then she went on talking. She could talk freely to nobody else in the world except this "demented" brother of hers.

"We're going to Gram's. She's Angel's mother and our family. You've got to behave or our Uncle Star might not take us. I mean it, Twig. You've got to hush up or I'll slap you so hard you won't know what hit you."

He did not understand the flood of words. Sometimes when he grew wild, nothing she did or said calmed him. He cried until he wore himself out. But this time, he hushed. Willow, seeing his eyes stray to the door, suspected she owed her success to the nice cop. Her brother was drawn to men Julius's age. He had never known his dad but he seemed to be forever searching for somebody like him.

She quit talking, did up his jeans, washed both their faces and hands and then went to work with the pocket comb. First she tugged it through Twig's springy curls. Even though his mop was too long and very dirty, it soon looked passable.

"No, no, NO!" he yelled at her finally, jerking away.

"Okay, cool it," she snapped.

Staring at herself in the mirror, she began wrestling with her own tangled mop. After she had the worst knots out, she drew the comb through more slowly, enjoying the way the teeth pulled through the last small snags and then slid freely all the way to the ends of her hair. One by one, every snarl gave way. If only everything would come straight that easily! And if only her hair, now it was combed, was as pretty as her little brother's. Instead it looked lank and lifeless.

"Forget that," she told herself sternly.

Yeah. You look like a million, Red Mouse put in. He could always be counted on to tell her how great she was even if she really wasn't.

"Thank you, Scarlet Rodent," she said silently, and went on with the task of tidying them up.

She straightened her jean jacket, tucked the envelope Angel had entrusted to Maisie back into her backpack and pulled Twig's cotton sweater down neatly. They wore no socks but they both had on worn sneakers which almost fit. That was something. Twig had not even had his until last week when Maisie had found them thrown out with somebody's garbage.

"All right, kiddo," Willow said softly, imitating her friend Sergeant Chang. "Let's go meet the tigers."

It was something she remembered Angel saying to her when she was small. Hand in hand, she and Twig walked out of the washroom. The constable was still there. Without bothering to ask, he hoisted Twig up onto his shoulders and led the way.

That man deserves a gold star, Red Mouse commented.

Two gold stars, Willow told him.

To her great relief, Sergeant Evans appeared to be leaving. She had her raincoat on and she was just closing the heavy door behind herself. She didn't wave goodbye or wish them luck. Willow pretended not to notice her. The nice cop took her place behind the desk. His grin almost cancelled her out.

Ms Thornton gave them a swift inspection.

"That's much better," she said gently. "Would you like some food while we wait?"

Willow looked at the policeman, smiled very faintly and shook her head.

"He got us food," she said.

Ms Thornton gave him an approving glance.

"Here's some more," the sergeant said, as a delivery kid came to the door. "Ham or cheese sandwiches. You can take your choice."

The children were halfway through eating when Uncle Star showed up. Willow remembered him at once, even though he'd grown from a teenage boy to a man. He looked like Angel, only with darker skin. His smile was dazzling.

"Hey, niece and nephew," he said, his bright eyes gleaming. "I'm Star. I remember Willow but I bet she doesn't remember me."

"I do," Willow said, rising and clutching Twig's hand. "You threw a Frisbee for me. This is my brother. He's called Twig."

"My sister named the poor kid Twig?" Star asked, shaking his head.

She hadn't. But Willow let it pass. Star showed Ms Thornton pictures of himself and Angel as children and his birth certificate.

"There's the very Frisbee I threw for her," he said, pointing at one snapshot and grinning at Willow.

They talked for a few minutes. Then Ms Thornton asked him what he was planning to do with them until the plane left.

"I'll call a cab and take them to my place," he said. "I can pick up some burgers or something and they can get cleaned up and maybe even sleep before we need to go to the airport.

It's only a little after six now. We don't need to be out there until after eleven."

His voice trailed off.

"I have a better idea," Ms Thornton said. "Let me drive you home now. We can stop by Woodward's and get the kids clean shirts, socks and underwear. You can see they have a bath and a nap and then I'll come by and drive you out to catch their flight. How does that sound?"

Star sighed with relief.

"Mostly it's okay not having wheels," he told her, "but this was looking complicated. A ride to the airport would make everything possible. Help buying them some clothes too would be great. They do look a bit scruffy. Thanks a lot."

Willow felt she should be insulted at being called scruffy when it was not her fault. Instead, she felt warmth stealing through her. Her uncle cared how she looked. Nobody had done that for months.

The caseworker and Star shook hands solemnly.

"Come on, gang," he said, holding out his hand to Twig. "Let's get moving."

Ms Thornton shepherded them out to her waiting Toyota. She and Star chatted as she drove to the clothing store.

"I think I can choose a few things," she offered. "You kids look too beat to shop. Wait here and I'll hurry."

She was incredibly fast. When she came back, carrying two bulging shopping bags, Twig was nodding off and Willow was sure she could not keep her eyes open another five minutes. They drove to Star's, scrambled out, promising to be ready when the social worker returned, and went up two flights to a small apartment.

Star's two rooms with a postage-stamp–sized bathroom were a palace compared to Maisie's. They were warm and clean. Star had put up bright posters on the walls and there were squashy, fat, yellow and orange and deep brown cushions tucked into the corners of the old couch and battered easy chairs. The bathroom had a toilet and a shower that worked. Willow was amazed that such luxury was for Star's use alone. In the fridge there was more food than Willow had seen in a long time.

Star put on a video he had picked up for them. Twig went to it at once like a homing pigeon. Never taking his eyes off the screen, he tucked his thumb in his mouth and became instantly engrossed. Maisie had not had colour TV. Willow, sitting beside him, watched him forget, in an instant, that she was there or that they were with a stranger. He was like Angel when she had just had a fix. Nothing else was as real; nobody else registered any longer.

Willow sighed. She could not forget. Even if she tried, she would not be able to escape from the emptiness and strangeness which kept threatening her. The Little Mermaid, which she had loved before, seemed shallow, all at once, and phony. Ariel, with her chirpy songs and her foolish yearning after Prince Eric, failed to touch Willow, who was longing for safety and sleep.

"Silly thing," she said to the swirling fishtail and red hair.

Her mind kept going around and around, wondering what Gram would think of her, of their scanty clothing, of Twig's strangeness. Finally, desperate for escape, she leaned her head back and shut her eyes.

Hush, little Willow, Red Mouse sang softly.

Star woke her almost an hour later.

"Pizza, anyone?" he called. Twig did not want to leave the video, so they let him eat his two slices, oozing with cheese, where he was. Willow sat with her uncle at a kitchen table. She was relieved to find that, friendly though Star was, he was too busy eating to keep prodding her with hard questions.

"I'll get Twig clean next," he said after gulping down his last big mouthful.

He pried Twig loose from the TV long enough to give him a quick shower. Twig was fearful at first, but Star went under the jet of water with him and turned it into a noisy game. When they came out, wrapped in towels, Star helped the little boy put on crisp clean jeans, new underwear, a T-shirt that read I'M A GREAT KID! and a warm, scarlet anorak with a hood and good deep pockets. Tucked into one sleeve was a pair of red socks. Willow stared at Twig in wonder. She could not ever remember seeing her brother dressed in such finery. He looked like a prince.

Twig loved his new clothes. He grinned, pranced about a little and then did a small pirouette so that Willow could view him from all sides. Then, weary from all that had happened since he got up, he collapsed on the floor and, glassy-eyed, went back to watching the images on the TV.

"You next, Willow," her young uncle said. "I left shampoo in there. Use all you want. Here's a comb."

"I have a comb," Willow told him, grateful all over again to the understanding policeman.

"Good. So go get started, Willow-tit-willow," he said, grinning at her.

Willow stared at him for one startled moment. She had been called that before, long ago. She did not have the energy to track down the memory, though. She stumbled into the tiny bathroom, stripped off her ragged clothes and stood under the stream of water until she could feel it beginning to cool. Then she hopped out, dried herself off and put on the things Ms Thornton had found for her. There was a hooded sweatshirt with a map of Canada on the front, a T-shirt with a lion cub on it, jeans like Twig's and underwear and socks. She pulled them on, marvelling at the thickness and softness of the various materials. She had not owned socks for months.

When she emerged, dressed and smelling sweet as the spring flowers at the market, she felt shy. But neither her uncle nor her brother noticed. A sleeping bag lay spread out on the floor next to the couch, where Twig was already asleep.

"Thanks," Willow said gruffly to her uncle. She held the arm of her new shirt up to her nose and once again sniffed its new, fresh smell. She felt exultant about these clothes. She and Twig would arrive in Ontario clean.

Star, watching her, grinned. Willow might not have much to say for herself but she was definitely pleased by what he and Ms Thornton between them had managed.

She tried to sleep, but a nagging question kept her awake in the darkness.

Red Mouse?

I am here, he said.

What about Gram? Will she keep us?

But for once Red Mouse had no answer. Finally, confronted

with silence and exhausted, Willow fell into an uneasy sleep. She dreamed Twig was lost and she was searching frantically for him. She could hear him calling out in terror but she could not find him. She wakened with a gasp and stared around the unfamiliar room. Where was she? Then she heard Twig breathing peacefully beside her and made herself lie still. She did not sleep again.

Star called them a couple of hours later. Willow scrambled up. They drank a glass of juice each and gobbled down a peanut butter sandwich. Breakfast would be served on the plane, but Star made them eat anyway.

Then Ms Thornton arrived and drove them all out to the airport.

"Good luck, Willow," said Star. "Bye-bye, Twig. Don't worry. Mum will be there to meet you. But here's her phone number in case something goes wrong."

He tucked a folded piece of paper into Willow's pocket and, along with it, a battered wallet which held some money.

Willow, to her own surprise, found herself hugging him fiercely. He hugged her back, ruffled Twig's hair and backed away. Ms Thornton stepped forward impulsively and kissed Willow's cheek.

"You are a brave girl, Willow Wind Jones," she said. "God bless you both. Now fly away home."

"Goodbye," Willow managed to get out. Her eyes stung with tears which she resolutely blinked away.

She hardly knew these people. It should not be so difficult to leave them. She raised her chin, clutched Twig with one hand, flung her backpack over her shoulder and turned to follow the lady who was waiting to escort them to the plane. She wanted to look back but she might cry if she saw them leaving. She must stay strong. Once she got started, she might not be able to stop. She had an ocean of unshed tears waiting to pour out.

"Come on," she growled at Twig and set out on the journey to Gram.

5
Up in the Air

"Is this your first flight, dear?" the woman taking them to the plane asked.

Willow nodded stiffly. Why hadn't she thanked Star and Ms Thornton? If they had not come to her rescue, she and Twig might already be in separate foster homes. She had heard plenty about foster homes from street kids who had run away from them. If even half the stories were true, she wanted no part of such places.

"I'd rather starve than go back," more than one had said.

There must be good ones. Lou had been a foster mother when she was younger. And Willow knew that Ms Thornton would never put children in families where they might be abused. The kids who lucked out didn't have to run, so she had not met them. But she didn't want to be put anywhere she might be separated from her brother.

Not only had Star and Ms Thornton saved them from

foster care, they had seen that they had been washed and fed and given clothes. Twig even had a little teddy bear which Star had given him at the last moment. When Gram met them, she would see two ordinary kids instead of two dirty, ragged orphans. It was wonderful.

"Where are you going?" the lady asked.

Twig didn't hear and Willow did not answer. The woman must know they were flying to Toronto. Where they went after that was none of her business. Getting mad over nothing helped keep Willow's jitters from growing into out-and-out panic. She marched along, step, step . . . step, step, tugging Twig in her wake, willing herself to forget that soon they would be far up in the air with no safety net beneath them.

"These two are travelling alone," the lady told the people on the plane. "They're the Jones children . . . Willow and Twig. Can you believe it?"

One flight attendant, a woman with milky skin, glossy red hair and wide, sparkling eyes, beamed down at Twig.

"Hi, honey-lamb," she cooed. "What a dear little bear you've got. What's your name really?"

Willow felt her cheeks burn.

"He can't talk yet. My name is Willow and his is Twig," she said, biting off the words.

"His name is what?"

"Twig." Willow repeated, speaking extra-loudly so that there would be no mistake. Twig's bottom lip was beginning to jut out dangerously. His sister gave up waiting to be taken to their seats and, turning right, pushed him ahead of her down the narrow aisle, searching for 26A and B. When she spotted them, she propelled him into the window seat. She was delighted when his attention was caught at once by the sight of two men getting a cage containing a large, mournful dog up into the hold. The dog howled and Twig laughed.

Without excusing herself, the sparkly-eyed flight attendant reached past Willow to do up Twig's seatbelt.

"Are those your Indian names?" she wanted to know.

This had happened before. The first few times, Willow had tried nodding, hoping that would end the discussion. But people always went on to ask what exactly their Indian names stood for or what their "real" names were.

"Our real names are Twig and Willow and our Indian names are Willow and Twig," she snapped, hoping to confuse the woman enough that she would give up.

Surely other passengers would soon be needing her attention. Willow wished they would hurry.

"Your little brother's such a cutie," the attendant gushed. If she had been able to reach Twig, she would have patted his curls. "You two don't look very alike?"

Willow leaned forward, putting herself squarely in the way. Twig did not like being petted and had been known to bite. She saw no reason to explain that they had different fathers.

"Is there a movie?" she asked. "Do we get to eat?"

Another attendant came up. Her smile lit up her eyes.

"Hi, Willow Jones," she said.

The phony lady turned to her and said sweetly, "I think somebody's a wee bit jealous of little brother. She doesn't want us paying too much attention to him. Isn't he a love?"

"Maybe," the nice one answered. "He looks tired and fed up to me. In answer to your questions, Willow, there is a movie and you do get a light snack now and breakfast later. If you need help, press this button and one of us will come. I'm Rhoda and this is Stephanie."

Willow gave Rhoda a guarded smile.

"Here come the other passengers," Miss Sparkler snapped, all her sweetness gone. "We must get to work. Press the call button if the child needs anything."

Willow snapped the buckle closed on her seatbelt and smouldered. How about her? She was only ten. Wasn't she a child too? And she wasn't jealous of her darling little brother.

She was so tired though that, once they were safely off the ground, she almost dozed off. Twig made real rest impossible though. Before they had been airborne fifteen minutes, he wriggled past Willow's knees and began to zip up and down the aisle.

Willow lunged to grab him as he shot past but he ducked out of her reach with ease. While she was unbuckling her seatbelt, he helped himself to a beer from the cart. Willow caught him and pried it loose from his clutching hands. Twig roared a protest.

The nice flight attendant helped her drag him back to their seats and brought him crayons and a little colouring book. Willow wished she could be all by herself with that book and those crayons and the neat little fold-down table. Twig scrawled red over every page and the table and then tried to eat the green crayon. Willow managed to get all the crayons back in their box and then, to keep them safe, she sat on them. Twig hit her, of course. He was furious. Willow let his small hard fist punch away at her right arm and wished the snack would come.

They were not the first to be served. When Twig saw people being handed trays of sandwiches and salad, he forgot the crayons. The nice flight attendant, seeing him struggling to get past Willow and snatch a meal for himself, hurried to bring them theirs ahead of the other passengers she should have served. For a good ten minutes, the two children ate in peace. Twig loved the slice of chicken in a bun. He polished off his dessert and would not touch the salad. Willow did not interfere. She was having too good a time savouring the meal.

Then Twig was squirming, trying to get out of his seat again. Miss Sparkler, looking disgusted, took his messy tray.

"You can have mine too," Willow said, knowing she'd need her hands free if Twig had nothing to do.

He had to pee. Willow didn't believe him but she took him to the tiny washroom at the very back of the plane. There didn't seem to be room enough for two in the confined space so she let him go in by himself. She reached in and helped him get his pants unfastened and then foolishly allowed him to close the door. He did pee. She heard the toilet flush twice. But he did not emerge. By the time she had forced the door open, he had sprayed soap all over himself. And the bathroom was festooned with toilet paper. He was holding a sanitary napkin when she yanked him out.

Rhoda came, like magic.

"Don't worry, Willow. I'll tidy up," she said. "Let's just wipe off a bit of the soap . . . "

Willow clutched Twig around the middle while the woman sponged him off.

"There, you little darling," she said, grinning at Willow.

57

"You look presentable. The movie will start in five minutes. I'm afraid he may find it scary. Can Twig hear, Willow?"

Nobody had ever asked Willow that before. She shrugged.

"He hears some," she said, and started towing her brother back past the staring, disapproving passengers.

They had just regained their seats when the captain told everybody there was going to be "a little turbulence" and they should do up their seatbelts. Willow was about to ask the Sparkler what "turbulence" was when the plane seemed to drop sickeningly. Then it bounced up and down. She opened her mouth to tell Twig not to worry when he threw up all of his snack. The Sparkler was not amused.

She muttered a word Willow knew well but was not expecting to hear in these surroundings. If she hadn't been busy trying to comfort Twig and mop him up, she would have laughed out loud.

He was frightened by the movie. Willow found it frightening too so she was on her brother's side when he began to scream and hide his eyes. You'd think the airline would remember that some of their passengers were small kids.

When, at long last, the plane was circling above the Toronto airport, Willow thought about Gram meeting the little darling, who still smelled of vomit, and she wanted to run away. But where?

"Stay in your seats when we land," the Sparkler told her. "Leave his seatbelt done up. We'll deplane you last."

Was that a real word, Willow wondered. Could you de-car or de-boat somebody?

She held Twig down. The small boy struggled but he

was too tired by this time to keep it up. They sat there, waiting to be collected, like parcels. When he rested his head against her shoulder and sighed wearily, Willow wanted to lift him onto her lap and rock him. Instead, she sat very still, giving him what time was left to rest.

"Here's the agent. He'll take you kids to whoever is meeting you," the Sparkler said, bored by them now.

If only Twig was not so messy! If only they didn't both smell of his vomit. If only she could summon up a happy smile, Willow thought, despairing.

Hey, you both look fine, Red Mouse said gently.

She knew it was not true but she was grateful. Gripping Twig's small, sweaty hand, she trailed after the agent.

"Have you got luggage?" the man asked.

Willow shook her head. She had her backpack and Twig's teddy bear safe. He, thank goodness, had been placed in the pocket of the seat in front of Twig and was still beautifully clean. He was the only one of them who looked as jaunty as he had when they left Vancouver.

What if nobody had come to meet them?

"Willow," called Gram's voice. It had an eager, loving note in it that made Willow's eyes smart.

And there was Gram herself, coming toward them with her arms out. She was a big woman with short white hair and glasses. Willow watched the wide smile grow even wider as she got close enough to see Twig's small sullen face and to catch a whiff of him.

"Hi, sweetheart," she said, leaning down to look into her grandson's eyes but not touching him.

Twig pressed closer to Willow and eyed this newcomer

narrowly. He did not know her. He had met too many strangers in the last twenty-four hours.

Gram did not push it. She turned to thank the agent. Then she reached out for Willow and, drawing her into her arms, ended up holding two children.

"Willow, poor Willow, you look worn to the bone," she said. "I know how it is. I flew across the country with Angel when she was only a month or so younger than Twig. She threw up twice!"

Willow stared up into the laughing face. She knew Gram. She knew her better than anyone. How could she have forgotten?

Twig didn't know her though. Willow braced herself for a scene. But he was too tired. He leaned against his grandmother and put his thumb in his mouth. He looked half asleep. It was going to be all right.

Then Gram really hugged her and Willow caught the shine of tears in her eyes. For the first time in what seemed like forever, Willow Jones let go of Twig's hand knowing her brother was perfectly safe. She hugged Gram back with all her strength. After a long, long time of waiting, Willow Wind Jones had come home.

6
The Road to Stonecrop

Gram began to lead the way to the parking lot. Twig staggered along, drooping with fatigue. Then Gram stopped and held out her arms. Twig, to Willow's astonishment, went to her. She lugged him all the way to the van. Willow walked so close beside her that she bumped into them several times.

"Don't worry, child. I won't lose you in the crowd," Gram said at last, with a laugh which was both understanding and breathless. Twig was heavy.

Willow tripped over her own feet. How had her grandmother guessed she was afraid of being separated from them and never finding them again? She had not known it herself until Gram spoke.

Gram went on walking, but a little more slowly. Twig roused on finding himself riding high. He stared around at the crowd but did not try to get down. Then the three of them reached the van. And there was a child's car seat in the back. Willow looked at it.

"Have you got kids?" she asked, as Gram let Twig slide to the ground and fitted her car key into the lock.

"Two of them, one named Willow and one named Twig," her grandmother said, boosting Twig into the van and starting to climb in to do up his seatbelt.

Twig pushed her hands away with an angry grunt.

Gram looked from his face, with its intent and impatient expression, to Willow's, which looked anxious.

"Does he want you to do it?" Gram began.

Click. The buckle snapped into place. Twig grinned triumphantly at them. Then he yawned so hugely Willow could see right down his throat.

"He learned in Lou's van. I guess he likes doing things for himself," Willow mumbled.

"Good. We like that attitude at Stonecrop," Gram said. "Just this once, you can sit up front with me."

Willow attempted to jump up into the high van seat but she was so tired. As she wobbled, one foot up and one foot down, Gram gave her a gentle boost. While Willow did up her own belt, her grandmother took her place in the driver's seat.

"Home again, home again, jiggety-jig," she said, and started the engine.

By the time they had merged with the traffic on the highway, Twig was fast asleep. He slumped sideways. He looked uncomfortable with his head dangling, but he was slumbering too deeply for them to disturb him.

"Did he sleep on the plane?" Gram asked.

"No," Willow said.

"Poor Willow," Gram said. "Nap now if you like."

Willow was so weary that every atom in her was crying out for sleep. Even so, she was in no danger of following her small brother's example. She had a dozen questions in her mind, lining up ready to be asked. If only she could get the information without sounding like Sergeant Evans! She hesitated. Where and how should she start? There was so much she didn't know . . .

"I can see you won't rest until you find out some things. Let me tell you a little about us," Gram said.

Willow waited.

But her grandmother did not go on. The pause lengthened. Why didn't she keep talking? Was something wrong? Had she changed her mind about Twig already? Was she taking them to a foster home? Willow sucked in her breath and her hands knotted in her lap.

Easy does it, Red Mouse told her. Don't get your knickers in a twist.

Lou had often said that. Willow relaxed fractionally.

"You will find our household . . . startling. You should be prepared . . . "

Willow waited as Gram paused again and then swore at a driver who tried to cut in front of her. No orphanage anyway. What did she mean by "household"?

They whizzed around a large truck.

"I was adopted by the Gordons when I was a baby and brought up at Stonecrop with Constance and Humphrey," Gram said.

"You were adopted!" Willow exclaimed. "I thought Angel . . . my mum . . . was adopted . . . "

"She was. After I married, my husband and I found we couldn't have children and we decided to adopt. I'd always wanted to anyway and he thought it was a great idea. So we adopted Angel and Star. She was four and he was a baby. When they were little, we lived in Toronto but we often visited my family at Stonecrop."

"Stonecrop . . . " Willow repeated softly. The word sounded so familiar, so strong.

"The Gordons came to Stonecrop as pioneers in 1841. When my father died, Mother couldn't farm the land so she sold off all but the farmhouse and the ten acres surrounding it."

"But what happened to your husband?" Willow said, wide awake now.

Gram laughed.

"It's complicated," she said. "I didn't mean to give you the whole family history before we got home."

"But I want to know," Willow said, surprised at herself. If she didn't know, how would she understand how she and Twig came into it?

"My husband had a heart attack and died when Angel was fifteen and Star eleven. A year later, I decided to bring the kids with me and come home to help care for Mother, who was unwell."

She paused. Willow made herself stay quiet. She stared out the car window at the fields, their ridges still white with snow. No mountains anywhere. No ocean either.

"Star was pleased but Angel begged to stay in Toronto and finish her year in high school. I shouldn't have let her, I guess. She was just sixteen. Well, she got pregnant. She came home and you were born. Stonecrop was your first home."

"My first home . . . " Willow echoed. She had thought she had never had a real home but maybe she had been wrong.

"Is your mother . . . ?" she started to ask.

"Mother died when you were about two. She left me and Humphrey and Con equal shares in the house. Humphrey wanted to stay. Con wanted out. So I sold my house in Toronto and Humphrey and I bought Con's share from her. Luckily, it has worked out beautifully for us both. Like Matthew and Marilla Cuthbert.

"I lived there too?" Willow asked, trying to get it straight.

"You lived there with us until you were about Twig's age," Gram said in a matter-of-fact voice.

Twig's age! Willow could not speak for a full minute. They drove along in silence, thinking their separate thoughts.

"Was Angel there too?" Willow said at last.

"She was there at first, going to school, but when you were a year old, she took off. She wanted to try living on the west coast. She left you with me, knowing how I loved you. She planned to come back in a few weeks. But it took her longer than she thought."

Willow was not at all surprised. It was a pattern she knew well. She drew in a breath but let it out without speaking. Gram waited a moment and then went on.

"She came back for you when you were nearly four. She had met a man she loved. He said you could live with them."

"Julius?" Willow asked.

"No. He came later. I forget the other one's name. Laird, I think. Or Land. Something like that."

"Laird," Willow said, remembering him. He had not lasted long.

"I didn't want to let you go, Willow, but she was your mother. And by then Star had gone west and found a job. I thought he might help keep an eye on you, but of course Angel was always on the move. I'm afraid we parted in anger, which is why she didn't bring you back even when she clearly should have done so. I told her that children weren't parcels to be left until called for. I said, if she took you, it must be for keeps. Me and my big mouth. My lecture kept me from seeing you until now. I imagine you've long since forgotten your life here."

"I remember some things," Willow said so softly her grandmother had to look to make sure she had spoken.

"You do? Are the memories good ones?"

Willow contented herself with a nod. She did not tell the woman beside her about the lighted Christmas tree which still shone in her mind. Or of Gram herself rocking her and singing lullabies. Or of running across a huge expanse of green grass to be caught up in Gram's arms.

She no longer wanted to listen to stories of the past though. What was going to happen today?

Gram seemed to understand.

"So that is how your Uncle Hum and I are still here, enjoying farm life," she said.

"Do you have cows?"

"No cows. Not yet. Hum keeps threatening to come home with one but I've warned him that, if he does, he'll have to milk her."

She laughed at that. Willow shot her a sideways glance. What was so funny?

"Wait until you see the set-up," her grandmother said

in answer to her unspoken question. "Stonecrop is no cottage. It's an old stone farmhouse, with ten acres of land, remember. The front lawn will look like a park to you. My old friends think I'm daft to be contented so far from civilization."

"How many rooms does it have?"

Gram was quiet, counting. Were there that many?

"There are five plus the porch and a small bathroom on the ground floor. On the second storey, there are three bedrooms and a big bathroom. Then there's the attic, which is really one large room, and the basement, which is three. How many is that?"

"Fourteen, I think," her granddaughter breathed. She could not remember ever having been inside a house that size. She had certainly never seen an attic and the only basement she had been in was the laundry room in one of Angel's friend's places. She had no notion how big an acre was. She felt bewildered.

"The first Gordons to live there, way before our time, called their home Stonecrop."

"They named the house?"

"Sure," Gram said. "They built it themselves. Will Gordon was a stonemason. Lots of the farms around us have names. Our area was settled by people from Great Britain. Most of them came from houses with names."

"Do you mean . . . just two people live in all those rooms?"

"Three people at the moment. Your Aunt Con moved in a couple of months ago. I'll tell you about her in a minute. But there's more than people. I've got my little Scottie

67

dog, Mrs. Tiggywinkle. We call her Tiggy for short. And Humphrey has his Seeing Eye dog Sirius. He's a black Lab. Then Con arrived with her two tiny papillons, Tobias and Pandemonium—called Toby and Panda for short."

Willow twisted once again to stare at her grandmother.

"You have four dogs?" she said, her mouth falling open.

Gram glanced at her, her hazel eyes twinkling behind her glasses.

"When I left home this morning, there were just four," she said solemnly.

Willow was dumbfounded. In her nearly eleven years of life, pets had never played a part. She did remember Angel rescuing a lost kitten or two but they always disappeared or somebody ended up taking them to the SPCA. Animals cost money and needed care. There had never been enough money or care to extend to a dog or permanent cat. Jo and Lou had had two big dogs but they had lived mostly outside and they were not fond of children. They were there to guard the two women living alone. Willow and Twig had both steered clear of them.

"What's Serious like? Why is he called that?" Willow asked at last.

"Sirius. You spell it S-i-r-i-u-s. He is a dog and he is a star and Sirius is the name of the dog star. He does also happen to be a very serious dog. He gets worried every time Humphrey is out of his sight. He clearly believes that, left alone, my brother hasn't a brain to bless himself with."

"Is he . . . Uncle Humphrey . . . blind then?" The words burst out before Willow had time to decide whether she should ask.

"He can see a little with one eye. But not enough to see cars coming. Not enough to read any longer."

"But I thought he wrote books. I found one with some stuff of my mother's. It says Humphrey Gordon right on the cover."

She stopped, not wanting to be rude, sure she must be making a mistake. She was also surprised to find herself talking almost freely to this stranger. Long ago, before they had been dumped at Maisie's, Willow had grown convinced that the safest thing she could do in a new situation was keep quiet.

"You're absolutely right. He is a writer. He writes with a talking computer. He'll show you how."

Willow wanted to know if this blind great-uncle had been pleased she and Twig were coming but she didn't dare ask that. She went over the phone conversations she had had with Gram the night before. Gram had never once said, "Wait till I talk it over with my brother and sister." She had simply said, "Come." And later, "Twig too. Of course, Twig too."

But if Uncle Humphrey or Aunt Con had doubts before they even met them, soon they were going to hate them. First they would not be able to stand Twig and his rages. They wouldn't take to his shrieks of excitement either. And they would not like her because she would always defend her brother no matter what.

Willow closed her eyes to stop the sting of tears. Then she yawned. Gram's big hand patted her knee.

"Rest, Willow Wind Jones," she said. "Sufficient unto the day is the worry thereof. We'll be fine. Remember that I'll be there to help. Now try to catnap. We have another forty minutes of driving."

Willow slid into sleep before she could stop herself. It was heavenly to let go, to give in to the enormous drowsiness which weighed down her eyelids. She half-wakened once to hear her grandmother singing softly beside her. She smiled, recognizing the words, and drifted off again.

"Deep in my heart, I do believe," Nell Jones sang to herself and her sleeping grandchildren, "we shall overcome someday."

7
The House
and Uncle Hum

"Wo, Wo!" Twig shouted.

Willow jerked awake. Where was she? Where was Twig? Then, turning her head sharply, she saw her brother in the rear-view mirror and her grandmother next to her at the same moment and remembered everything. In the next second, she understood why Twig had called to her. The van had left the road and was heading down a long farm lane, lined with piles of melting snow. At the far end, a towering stone house watched their approach through its tall windows. It was set amid dark evergreens and other leafless trees. For an instant, it looked bleak and forbidding. Then the sun came out and it was transformed.

"Willow and Twig, welcome to Stonecrop," Gram said, and switched off the engine.

Willow sat very still, staring. She had thought Stonecrop

would be utterly strange to her, but she remembered this place. She had been here before and she had felt safe here, safe with her Gram. Was this where she had seen that Christmas tree? In Vancouver, there were no houses like this. She had seen a few big stone houses in pictures and on TV at Jo and Lou's. But they were as remote from her life as castles or pagodas. And yet, the moment she saw it, Stonecrop was home.

I remember you, house, she thought. I remember you.

She had never returned to a beloved place. She had been dragged from Laird's bachelor apartment to a trailer to a dirty room high up in a boarding house. Then Julius had come into their lives and they had moved in with him. That had been a joyous time for Willow. But then Julius had taken off and they had been homeless again.

Willow had been frightened then. But before long, her mother had called her friends Jo and Lou and they had fetched them. Until the baby arrived, she and her mother had lived with the two women in their remote cabin. A few days after Twig's birth, Angel had gone, too, leaving a note to say she would be back soon. Before Willow saw her again, over two years had passed.

In that cabin way up north Willow had had to care for Twig a lot but Lou had sent for correspondence courses and Willow had also learned to read and do basic math. Jo and Lou had lots of books. She had read anything she liked. Most of them had been written for grown-ups but not all. The women complained every so often about Angel's kids but they had been kind. They might be there still if Lou's brother had not moved in and started hitting Twig every time the small boy did not look at him or answer him. Then Lou had gotten them out of bed, while he was in a sound sleep, and packed them into her jeep and taken them back to Vancouver. She somehow located Angel and the two children were returned to their mother along with a lecture about getting off the drugs and taking responsibility for her kids.

"I will, I promise," Angel had said.

But Willow had known, by then, what that sort of promise was worth. Twig, uprooted and hurt, had driven his mother crazy. A couple of months later, Angel herself had handed them over "temporarily" to Maisie. Nowhere they had lived had felt the least bit safe except for the cabin and it, in the end, had turned out to be the least safe of all.

Willow thrust the troubling memories away and came back to the present. Inside Stonecrop, there was what sounded like an army of roaring dogs. They all barked at once. It sounded like more than four. Hearing the uproar, Willow tensed, trying to think of how best to introduce her brother to a pack of strange dogs.

Then Twig laughed. She loved his laugh. It was deep and husky and very contagious. She had not heard it much lately. She looked to see what was making him chortle and caught sight of two dogs in one of the front windows. They were very small with large ears standing up like wings. As she gazed, they were joined by a stocky black Scottie with a whiskery face and jutting eyebrows. Twig laughed harder and he positively shrieked when a huge Lab jumped up on something, a couch or a chair maybe, under the window and peered out over the heads of the other three.

"Come on, you two. Let's go in. They'll be deafening poor Humphrey with their barking," their grandmother said.

As Willow slid her feet to the ground, she went on watching the front of the house. She was nervous, not about the dogs but about Uncle Humphrey and Aunt Con. Were they going to come out to say hello to them? How did you greet a blind great-uncle anyway?

"Shut up. Quiet, you numskulls! Stop that noise right this instant! QUIET!" someone inside was bellowing.

Could those roars be coming from the old blind writer? Willow didn't think so. She waited for the dogs to cower and stop their racket. But not one of them paid the slightest attention to the shouted commands. They all barked on hysterically as though their master had failed to realize people were coming up the front walk and they would lose their steady jobs if they neglected to warn him. It was insane.

It was also funny. Twig was shrieking with glee and Willow found herself actually giggling.

All at once, as they approached the door, their laughter stopped. Twig clutched Willow's hand, needing to make sure she was there to protect him from whatever was coming. His bright eyes watched the big door. As they neared the glassed-in front porch, Willow saw, perched on the peak of the roof, a large bird in flight.

"It's a blue heron weathervane," Gram told her, pulling the porch door open. "The wind is blowing from the south. That's a good sign."

Then they were inside the porch. It was a small room in itself, with windows on both sides and in the outer door. Even though it was still wintry here in Ontario, there was a pattern to the tiles which made a flower in the centre of the floor.

"Twig, look," she said, pointing to the flower design,

trying to delay the frightening moment when they would have to face whoever was in there, beyond the porch.

"It's a message for you," Gram said. "It says, 'Bloom here, my children.'"

Twig's eyes were still fixed on the inside door. Gram opened it and strode into a hurly-burly of leaping, yelping dogs. There seemed to be far more than four of them.

"Hello, Wild Things. Let the Wild Rumpus cease!" Gram told them, leaning down to pat first one and then another. "Quiet! It's only me, you brainless beasts."

The barking diminished very slightly. Gram turned to the children, who stood pressed close to each other, their eyes wide.

"They won't hurt you, I promise. They're foolish but they're friendly."

Twig and Willow stood wavering, wanting to do the right thing but having no notion of how to approach this motley crew of mutts. Behind the dogs, almost unnoticed, stood Uncle Humphrey.

"Hold out your fingers for them to sniff," Gram instructed. "They won't nip. They just want to learn your scent."

Willow, avoiding looking at the silent man, went down on one knee and, with her heart pounding, extended her closed fist. She was too fond of her fingers to risk them so soon. She kept her other arm around her brother, who was bouncing up and down on the balls of his feet and emitting small, wordless shrieks. When her hand was sniffed and then bathed by several dog tongues, he plopped down next to her and offered them both his hands with all ten fingers spread out.

"Hi! Hi!" he said, using one of his few words. "Hi! Hi!"

Not one of the small fingers was bitten off. Twig giggled at the feel of so many soft tongues in three sizes. The papillons' felt like twins.

By the time dog-greeting was completed, Willow had managed to sneak a good look at her great-uncle. Uncle Humphrey did not resemble anyone else Willow knew and yet he looked as familiar as Gram. He was tall, a head taller than his sister. His brown hair, streaked with grey, was cut short. He was thin and bony. His eyes, though clouded, were blue-grey. Willow had no idea whether he could see her or Twig, but he was facing in their direction. Just in case he could see more than Gram had said, she gave him a shy smile.

Uncle Humphrey did not see or, if he did, he did not smile back directly at her. He smiled generally, not looking right at anyone. But he did seem friendly. It was a good smile. And a familiar smile. She knew it as well as she knew Twig's.

"Here they are," Gram said to him. "The bigger one is Willow and this fellow is Twig. Is he called Twig because he always has a tight hold on you, Willow?"

Willow nodded and braced herself for all the rest of the questions about names.

But Gram did not ask them. She waited for her brother to speak. He did so, sounding slightly tense.

"Hi, Twig. Hello, Willow. How's Red Mouse these days?"

She stiffened for one second before she took in the sound of his voice. She could not believe her ears. Uncle Humphrey had Red Mouse's voice. She had known Red Mouse always and she had come to believe she had invented him herself. But it had been this man.

"He's fine," she said in a dazed voice. Then she had to know.

"How did he begin?" she asked.

"You said, 'Tell me a story, Uncle Hum.' I said, 'What about?' You said, 'About a red mouse.' I said, 'What's his name?' You were sitting on my lap so I could see your face and you looked at me as though I'd lost my marbles and you said, 'His name is Red Mouse, of course.'"

"I remember!" Willow cried, her usually guarded expression giving way to a look of delight. Now she understood, at last, why Red Mouse talked like a grown-up. He had this great-uncle's laugh too.

My laugh is my own, I'll have you know, Red Mouse told her tartly.

For once, Willow ignored him. She went on talking. "Oh, I do remember. You made up his seven sisters . . ."

Uncle Hum chuckled, as pleased as she was. "Scamper, Scoot, Scurry, Skip, Skedaddle and . . . there must be two more."

"Skeezix," Willow chimed in. "Red Mouse likes Skeezix best. She's pink and she can fly."

"What a memory!" her uncle said admiringly. "Now let's get a better look at this brother of yours."

Uncle Hum came closer and leaned down to gaze at Twig. The little boy was staring first at Willow's face and then up at Uncle Hum's. He could not understand what was being said but he was startled by Willow's joy. He was also disturbed by it. He had seen her look loving and angry, tired and worried, stubborn and fearful. But rarely had he seen her light up like this.

He pushed in between her and the strange man, reminding her that she was his.

Willow knew how he felt. She hugged him against her. Catching his tension, she once again braced herself for whatever he would do next.

Uncle Hum saw a lot for somebody who was supposed to be blind. He backed away two or three steps and straightened up.

"Are you two hungry?" he asked, as though Twig had greeted him politely.

"We ate on the airplane," Willow said in a half-whisper. "But it was quite a while ago and Twig threw up afterwards."

"Are you hungry now, Twig?" Uncle Hum persisted.

Willow pulled her small brother around so that he could see her face. She repeated the word "hungry" and patted her stomach.

Twig nodded, his face splitting into a grin.

"Waffles should hit the spot," Uncle Hum said, and he began moving toward the kitchen.

"Has Con phoned?" Gram asked him as she and the two children followed. "Did you warn her?"

"She did not call us. Maybe this will teach her to leave us a number where she can be reached. We would certainly not over-use it. I heard her say, before she took off, that she thought she'd be back on Friday sometime. So we'll have a big surprise for her when she shows up."

It's only Thursday, Willow thought. Yesterday morning, Maisie was alive.

She pulled her thoughts in as though they were runaway horses. It would not be good to think of Maisie right now.

"Knowing Con, I think 'shock' might be a better word," Gram said. "Trust Constance not to be available when she's wanted. Let me show the kids where they'll sleep and give their hands and faces a wash while you get the batter mixed up. Make enough for me too. I hope Twig likes waffles."

Willow had had waffles but she was pretty sure Twig had never tasted them. She was positive he would like them. She herself had loved them. She nodded.

"Your uncle can't see you nod," her grandmother said quietly. "You'll have to remember to say yes or no when you're talking to him. Willow loves waffles, Hum. I can tell by the smile."

"Good," Uncle Humphrey said. "I'll plug in the waffle iron."

He entered the kitchen, followed by Sirius, Toby and Panda. Tiggy stuck close to Gram and eyed Twig uneasily. Willow felt confused. Uncle Hum did not walk as though he couldn't see where he was going. She was also curious about what a waffle iron was. She was sure waffles came out of a package and were heated up in a toaster. She was positive they were not ironed. They had little holes all over them. Nobody ironed food.

"Follow me," said Gram, and headed up the stairs that rose straight up out of the front hall.

There were twenty steps to go up. Beside them a wooden banister rose. Willow ran her hand up its smooth surface. She had heard of sliding down banisters. This must be the right kind. The wood, although scarred here and there, was slippery and wouldn't snag on pants.

For one instant, she imagined she saw a fair-haired girl in

79

a long old-fashioned dress standing at the top looking down at them. Then she blinked and the girl was gone. It must have been a trick of the light.

Twig clung to her hand but his eyes were wide as he tried to take in, in one moment, so much that was wonderful and alien to him. Far above them, on the hall ceiling, there were painted plaster flowers and leaves. He squeezed her fingers and pointed up. She nodded.

As she did, she realized how hard it was going to be to remember to speak each time she wanted Uncle Hum to understand she meant yes or no. Twig was the very opposite of their great-uncle. Unless she nodded or shook her head, he mostly missed her meaning. They had a whole language they had invented made of gestures and facial expressions and a small handful of words. He could hear something. She listed off, inside her head, the sounds he used for his few words. "Wo" for Willow. "Doin'" for "What are you doing?" "Eat" for "I'm hungry and want something to eat." "Wa-wa" for "water" or anything he wanted to drink. And "Hep" when he needed her help. She had also managed to collect and carry with her a grubby, half-torn envelope filled with pictures she'd ripped out of an old Sears catalogue she'd found at Jo and Lou's place. She had sought out other pictures in the junk mail that was delivered to Maisie's building. She only got the envelope out when they were alone together and it was getting very worn. In it were pictures of people, clothes, a car, a dog, a door, shoes and boots, a piano, a teddy bear, a slide, a small chalkboard, various foods, a fire truck, a dump truck, and one of two children hugging each other. By now, Twig could tell when she meant certain things without getting out the pictures. Even though he did not say more than a dozen words, and those all incomplete, his actions showed he understood. He was beginning to read her lips too.

"I love you, Twig," she could say and he would put his arms around her and hug her like the little boy in the picture.

Maisie had called him "the poor little retard" or "dumb brat" sometimes. But Willow had never let her see the pictures. It was her secret, hers and Twig's.

At the top of the long staircase, the two children followed Gram into a room on the right and stood transfixed. It was a bathroom. But it was almost as big as Maisie's whole living space. The floor tiles looked like smooth mottled stone. The walls were deep green. And there were two enormous windows looking down over a long gentle hillside to fields and, at the bottom, what looked like a creek. The windowsills were deep enough for the kids to sit in and even pull their feet up after them.

"Pee," Twig said, pointing excitedly to the toilet.

"Good idea," Gram said. "I'll wait outside."

Willow hardly noticed her departure. She was staring at the bathtub, which was long and oval and shining clean. It had special things which she later learned made it a Jacuzzi. And it had a shower on a cord like a telephone so you could lift it down. On the edge of the tub, three bright yellow rubber ducks, big, medium and small, sat, ready to go swimming with a child. There was a boat, too, with a thing for winding it up.

"Wo," Twig yelled, pounding on her leg. "Wo, pee."

"Sorry. Okay, okay," his big sister said and unfastened

his jeans. She lifted the wooden toilet seat up for him and watched him trickle a little stream. She had known he did not have to go badly but she did not mind. Toilet training him was one of the best things Jo had done for her.

When he was finished, she did him up and went herself. Gram had left them alone, giving them privacy. But privacy had not been possible at Maisie's, where there was only a small room with a door that would not lock. Behind the door was the single toilet, minus its seat, and a sink. Everyone who lived along the hall used the same bathroom. You were supposed to knock and listen before you opened the door, but some of the people in the building were too old or too stoned to remember. The room stank. To Willow, the shining cleanliness of this new bathroom was as wonderful as the marble floor and the view.

She took Twig over to the basin and turned on the taps. Soon the gushing water grew warm and then piping hot. Brother and sister smiled at each other, rinsed their fingers and were about to dry them on the seats of their jeans when Gram came back in.

"Here are your towels," she said, pointing.

They each had a big fat bath towel, a smaller hand towel and a washcloth. Twig's were bright red and Willow's a soft fleecy yellow. They looked so new and beautiful that Willow hesitated, not wanting to spoil them. Twig had no such doubts. He dried his hands thoroughly.

"Let me give your faces a bit of a wash," Gram said softly. Willow stiffened. They could wash their own faces. Then she caught her grandmother winking at her. What did she mean by that? Willow caught on as Gram soaped the yellow washcloth first and washed her face thoroughly from hair-line to collarbone. It felt marvellous. Willow, drying herself, beamed down at her brother.

Twig, watching through narrowed eyes at first, saw the smile and held up his face when Gram had the red washcloth ready. He was a shade or two lighter when she finished, especially his neck and ears.

"This is bigger than any other bathroom in the world," Willow said, feeling a hard jolt of anger as she thought again of the meagre, smelly room at Maisie's.

"It used to be a bedroom. But never mind it now. Let me show you your rooms," Gram said, going ahead of them again.

Willow trailed after her, but her steps dragged. She and Twig had always slept together, in the same bed at first and then, at Maisie's, in sleeping bags pulled close enough for Twig to reach out and touch her if he needed to. If Gram was going to insist he sleep in a separate room, she was sure he would have a purple fit. And the minute he did that, screaming and kicking and punching and even biting anyone who came near enough, Gram would start looking for somewhere else to send them.

"I thought you'd be used to sleeping in the same room," Gram said lightly. "So you can share until Twig gets big enough to want his own place. You can sleep in the top bunk, Willow, and Twig can sleep in the bottom."

The heaviness inside Willow dissolved. The bunk beds were already made up. She showed Twig his. It wasn't hard to tell. He had a comforter with prancing wild animals on it, pink hippos, green giraffes, baby blue elephants and scarlet lions.

"Wo, Wo," he said excitedly. "Wook!"

Willow grinned at him. Then she climbed the end of the bunk, which had been made into a solid ladder. Her comforter was as lovely as his but it had trees and birds on it. It was not new like her brother's. The soft, printed fabric was worn in places. She was sure she had seen it before. She studied it and then she looked down at her grandmother, who was smiling up at her.

"Do you see what kind of trees they are?" Gram asked.

Willow looked down at the comforter again. She did not know the names of trees.

"They're willows," her grandmother said. "It was Angel's when she was your age. She loved it so much that I've always kept it. I couldn't tell if there was a wind blowing the branches but I thought of the quilt the moment Angel told me she had named her baby Willow Wind. When you lived with me, it was in your crib."

Willow tried to speak but she couldn't. Slowly, she came down to the floor again. She made another attempt to tell Gram how special everything was, most of all her mother's comforter, but the words stuck in her throat.

Twig had no such problem. He jumped out of the bottom bunk and hugged Gram's legs.

"Why, thank you, Twig," Gram said, her hand brushing his curly head.

"I . . . " Willow tried, her tongue still unco-operative. "I want . . . "

"I know," her grandmother said, putting her hand on her granddaughter's thin shoulder. "I know, Willow. You needn't say a word. Let's go up now to the attic. When you're ready, it'll be your special place." ·

"The waffle batter is ready when you are," Uncle Hum's deep voice called from the floor below.

"We'll be right down," Gram called back. "Willow, you can explore the attic after we eat. I have a feeling you've seen enough for now anyway."

She went ahead of them down the stairs. Willow and Twig followed hand in hand. The Scottie brought up the rear, thumping down each step.

"Wo," Twig said, squeezing her fingers. "Wo . . . "

"I know," Willow murmured, squeezing back.

Then they were in the kitchen and it was time for the waffles. Twig, getting over his awe, chose that moment to begin chasing the dogs, shrieking with excitement as they fled. The black Lab stood his ground one second too long, unable to believe that a small boy could so suddenly become so wild.

Wham! Twig slapped him on the head as hard as he could.

"NO!" Willow cried out. "Oh Twig, don't."

He didn't hear her, of course. He would not have cared if he had. But Gram stopped him. She grabbed hold of him, gave him a sharp shake, lifted him bodily into a wooden high chair and plunked him down without ceremony.

"That's enough of that," she said in a cold strong voice Willow was sure Twig heard. "Now act like a boy instead of a wild animal and you can have waffles along with the rest of us. Serve them up, Hum, spit-spot."

Twig, rigid and trembling, glared at his grandmother but he sat still for the moment. And Willow, feeling as though her worst nightmares were about to come true, slid onto the chair next to him.

"Willow, don't look like that," Gram said, her coldness gone like magic. "Remember that the darkest hour comes just before the dawn."

Willow had been examining the grain in the wooden table. Her head jerked up. Then the dread in her eyes glimmered into a faint smile.

"When does the dawn get here?" she asked.

"Any minute now," Gram said and, stooping, kissed her granddaughter on the top of her head.

8

Gram Guesses

Willow took hold of Twig's right foot and held on tight to let him know she was right there. Then she saw that his rage was already melting away as he stared around yet another new room.

She looked around too, uncertain what was going on. Where were the waffles? She saw no cardboard box. In its stead, she caught sight of a large, rectangular grill sort of thing steaming.

"What's that?" she asked.

"It's a waffle iron," Uncle Hum said, his tone surprised.

"Twig, sit still," Gram said, restraining him as he began to climb out of the high chair. He wiggled under her firm hand and glowered up at her but he did not go on struggling. The food smelled far too good.

Willow, her eyes wide, watched. Did waffles come from a cooker kind of thing? Uncle Hum, moving slowly and bending down to peer closely at what he was doing, spooned more of the batter into the waffle iron and closed the lid. Twig hiccoughed but stayed where he was. He was distracted by the waffle-making. Willow had learned, long ago, that reasoning with Twig rarely worked but distracting him often did.

Uncle Hum had set the waffle iron up well out of Twig's reach but, when the lid began to lift slightly, revealing the golden waffle, the small boy pointed at it.

"Wo, wook! Wook!" he shouted.

Willow reached out and clasped his hand. But her gaze, too, was glued to the sight of the waffle.

Then, out of the corner of her eye, she saw Uncle Hum touch his wrist watch.

"It is nine-o-three a.m.," a small tinny voice said quite clearly.

Willow jumped and stared at the talking watch. Twig obviously had not heard it. He went on watching the waffle.

"It has stopped steaming, Hum," Gram said.

"It should be perfect," Uncle Hum said briskly and lifted the lid all the way up. The golden waffle was on the roof of the waffle iron and had to be gently pried free.

"It takes exactly four minutes in this one," their great-uncle explained. "The other waffle iron we have is bigger but much slower."

He divided that first waffle in two, giving half to each of the children. Gram buttered Twig's and began pouring on corn syrup. Suddenly recalling he was angry at her for picking him up so roughly, Twig shot out his fist, knocking the syrup bottle flying.

"Don't you like syrup?" Gram asked, deftly fielding the

bottle and putting it out of his reach. "How about some jelly?"

This time she held out two bottles so that he could choose. He could not read. But, scowling at her, he pretended to scan the labels. Then, with a quick, anxious glance at his sister, he pointed to the red currant jelly.

Willow was furious. She hated their grandmother all at once. Twig would love the syrup better than some dumb jelly. He had not meant to give up his chance at tasting it.

She glared at the woman about to spoon jelly onto his waffle and said in a low, grating voice, "Twig wants syrup."

Gram paused, her hand with its spoonful of jelly still in mid-air.

"But Willow," she said in a firm, reasonable tone, "you saw him knock the—"

"He didn't know," Willow protested hoarsely, her head bent over her own plate. "He's never tasted syrup. It wasn't fair. He didn't know . . . "

She choked. She had no idea why she felt this boiling rage against the woman who had rescued them. She would have hit Gram if she had dared, hit her harder than Twig had done.

"Nell," Uncle Hum said quietly, lowering the lid of the waffle iron on more rich batter, "Willow has always looked after Twig. She knows best, don't you think? I know you are the experienced mother around here but I don't think you should start in on your perfect child-rearing methods quite so soon. Let his big sister help him, for God's sake."

Gram's cheeks reddened. Without a word, she passed Willow the bottle of syrup. Willow shot her great-uncle a wondering, thankful look which he could not see but seemed to sense. Then she tapped Twig's hand. He turned and stared at her, his pupils dilated, panic written all over him.

"Twig, try this," his sister said loudly and clearly. "Open your mouth."

She forked up a bite of her own waffle, with butter and syrup on it, and held it out to him. Twig opened his mouth like a baby bird, gulped down her offering and smiled stickily.

"I'll give you some," she said, tipping the syrup bottle so that a thick stream ran onto his waffle. Before he could start eating it with both hands, she hastily put down the bottle and began cutting his waffle up into bite-size pieces. Then she gave him the spoon.

He went at the delicious food as though he had not eaten anything for weeks. Willow turned, head averted, back to her own plate. She waited, her face half-hidden by her long bangs. Was Gram still angry?

"Well done, you two," Gram said. The red that had stained her cheeks at her brother's words faded. "I wasn't thinking. You'll both have to help me."

"Don't worry," Uncle Hum said, grinning at her. Then he put an entire waffle on a plate and gave it to her. "Eat. You didn't have anything before you took off this morning, like a kid going to the circus."

Gram raised her head, smiled broadly and began eating as though she, too, were ravenous. When all of them were stuffed, Gram wiped the children's hands and faces with a wet paper towel. Twig squirmed slightly but ended up letting her clean him off. Then she started to pull his chair back. Twig hunkered down in it, clutching the arms and refusing to get down. He was going to be obstinate.

Willow was having none of that. She wanted to explore. Not only had she never seen a waffle iron before, she had never seen an attic either.

"Come on," she told her brother, trying to yank him free of the chair.

For one moment, Twig balked. Then the look in her eye plus his own need to make a voyage of discovery around this strange new place made him give in and he landed bouncing on his two feet. He was ready for the next adventure.

"I'll clear up," Uncle Hum said. "You take them on the rest of the guided tour. Watch out for that stray orange cat. He sneaked in the dog door and ran up the stairs while you were away. The dogs met him in the upstairs hall and chased him down again. At least, I believe that's what they were doing when they came close to knocking me flying. I could hear the cat yelling insults at them from that old platform in the pear tree. He's got guts. He'll probably try his luck again, dogs or no dogs."

"A stray cat we do not need," Gram said, and ushered the children out.

We're strays, Willow thought uneasily.

But not cats, Red Mouse remarked.

Gram showed them the den, a room with two more big windows and hundreds of books. Off it was Uncle Hum's small study where he wrote his children's novels and poems.

"It was the birthing room when the first Gordons built it," Gram said. "Elspet Mary Gordon, their adopted daughter, wrote a book here in a big farm ledger. It's our most cherished family heirloom. I think you'd like it."

"What's a birthing room?" Willow asked, trying to act

interested even though she really wanted to see the attic instead.

"It's a special room on the ground floor where women could give birth and people who were ill or dying could be nursed by their family."

"Lou had a book called *The Borning Room*," Willow said.

"It's the same thing," Gram told her. "Hum thinks it makes a perfect writing room because his imagination gives birth to all sorts of people in there. And sometimes he even kills somebody off. And he claims he is sometimes visited by Elspet Mary's ghost."

Willow remembered the moment when she had glimpsed an old-fashioned girl in the upstairs hall. It had just been a trick of the light though, not a ghost. She was almost certain.

They continued their tour. Next came the dining room with its beautiful dark wooden table and, after that, a big bright room they had had built on at the back.

"We call it the West Wing," Gram said, smiling.

But she rushed them a bit. She clearly wanted to show Willow the attic as much as Willow wanted to see it.

They paused long enough on the second floor to glance in at Gram's and Aunt Con's rooms. Again there were tall windows with deep sills. And the rooms themselves were spacious and inviting.

Yet they were so different. Gram's was comfortable, a bit messy, but not one bit fancy. Sunlight streamed through the windows, lighting piles of books on the bed and on the floor. There was a goose-necked reading lamp with a green shade and the duvet cover was patterned with earthy colours— browns, greens and the deep red of poppies. The bed was old and had a large carved headboard and a curving footboard. Aunt Con had a much bigger bed with no head or foot. It wore a sort of frilly skirt, a pretty spread and matching pillows with ruffled pillowcases. Even the curtains matched. They seemed to be the only ones in the house. On a small table next to the bed lay two books. One looked like a diary. It had a tiny padlock. The other was underneath so Willow could not see its title. On the floor next to this bed lay a large basket full of coloured tapestry threads and an embroidery hoop with a picture of a puppy on it. Only his head was finished but the sewing was beautifully done.

Gram saw Willow's look of surprise and laughed.

"She's determined to be ultra-feminine," she said. "You'll see when she arrives. We three are all very different but Con still amazes me with her fripperies. Her embroidery is expert though. I do well to patch jeans and sew on buttons. Come on."

Willow looked at Gram in her sweat shirt, jeans and work boots and grinned. Twig had run over to the window and was looking out into an apple tree. A red-breasted bird sat on a high branch and gazed back at him.

Gram's eyes followed his just in time to see the bird take flight.

"Oh, there's the robin," she said. "He must be planning to settle down and build his nest around here. He's the first. I'm sure he's the same one I've been catching sight of all week. I know they aren't the same as the English robin in *The Secret Garden* but they always are special to me because of that bird. Have you read *The Secret Garden*, Willow?"

Willow shook her head. She was happy Twig had seen a

robin but she stayed by the door as a hint to her grandmother. Gram saw what she was up to and speeded up
slightly.

"Now for the attic," she said.

About time, Red Mouse said rudely. Willow was glad only
she could hear him. The narrow stairs leading up to the third
floor curved around at the bottom and then went straight up.
The steps were steep and uncarpeted and the banister was
narrow, too, and rattly. But at the top, Willow gasped and
stood stock-still.

A long room stretched off to her left and right. There
were two casement windows at each end and three skylights
in the ceiling. Through them, she saw thin shafts of sunlight
slanting through the tumbling grey clouds. The ceiling sloped
down the length of the room, although not to the floor.

A dusty screen that looked Chinese blocked off the right
hand end of the bare chamber. The space behind it was
almost a room in itself.

"Someday, if you wish, Willow," her grandmother said,
"you can create a private kingdom here."

Willow tiptoed around the screen. This end of the room
held a narrow bed with a couple of pillows, a bookcase with
three old books and a child's rocking chair.

Twig pushed past her, glanced around and ran back to
the larger empty space where he could race around in thun-
derous abandon. His sister ignored him. He would keep it
up until he was deserted or until he grew tired. She moved
forward soundlessly, her eyes wide with wonder. There was
a picture on the wall of children playing hide-and-seek
amid some trees. She went closer and touched it softly

with her fingertip. Someone had painted it. It wasn't a copy. It looked old.

"We think Elspet Mary painted that picture," Gram said. "Those are her initials. You don't have to keep it up here. I thought you might like it. Hum swears she haunts the place."

"I like it a lot," Willow murmured under Twig's racket.

She went to examine the books. They were called *Eight Cousins*, *The Secret Garden* and *Emily of New Moon*. Her heart leapt. She had read none of them.

Twig stopped to watch her. She dropped the book she was holding and turned away without showing her excitement. He had torn apart a book when they first came to Maisie's, because she got so taken up with it that she stopped paying any attention to him. It had been a battered copy of *Alice's Adventures in Wonderland* which Maisie had picked up for her at a rummage sale. But when Twig had finished with it, it had been nothing but a pile of ripped-up rubbish.

"You can come back any time you like," Gram said gently into the silence. "Angel loved that painting, by the way. Now let's go down."

A warm glow spread through Willow. Gram spoke of her daughter with love. Everyone else Willow knew was fed up with her. Maisie and Jo and Lou and some of the others who had come and gone before them often swore when Angel's name came up. Willow was used to being spoken of as one of "Angel's brats" and knowing that she and Twig were a burden. She understood, even shared, their anger. But it was healing to hear her mother spoken of with love.

"Where does Uncle Hum . . . Humphrey sleep?" Willow asked.

"In the basement. He has his own private kingdom down there. A bedroom, bathroom and sitting room. I'm sure he'll gladly show you around."

Then Gram eyed her two grandchildren appraisingly. "I think you must be tired. It's only eleven o'clock but your systems are still on Vancouver time. So it feels like eight. How about a bath and a nap?"

Willow nodded gratefully. She was sagging with weariness. Although Twig had snored contentedly in his sleeping bag on Uncle Star's floor, she had lain awake most of the time, trying to think what she would do if this grandmother turned out not to want them after all. She knew it could happen. Even yet, they had not seen Twig at his worst . . .

He had galloped down both flights of stairs ahead of them. Just as they reached the second floor, a startled yelp and then a shriek shattered the comfortable, quiet sounds of a peaceful house. The whole pack of dogs came racing up the stairs as if the devil himself were after them. But it was Twig who was chasing them, screaming his lungs out. And Uncle Hum was bringing up the rear, his face red with anger, his quiet voice raised as he struggled to be heard above the racket.

Willow jumped into her brother's path and grabbed him around the middle. Then she deliberately toppled backwards so that she would not be dragged down the stairs. Gram shooed the dogs into the bathroom and shut them in.

"He was chasing them," Uncle Hum puffed, giving Twig a baleful stare. Even though he did not see Twig clearly, he had no trouble locating him by the rumpus he was raising. "He grabbed Tiggy's tail first but she escaped. Then he picked

Toby right up off the ground by *his* tail. Sirius went to Toby's rescue, growling like a lion and looking as dangerous as such a gentle dog could. He didn't bite but he charged and barked and the boy dropped Toby. But, the next instant, he was off after them again . . . "

"Oh, Twig," Willow moaned, clutching her brother's thrashing body. "Oh, Twig, how could you?"

Nobody heard her. Her ears rang and her heart felt squeezed into a tight ball. What was going to happen next? Then, as abruptly as a siren being turned off, Twig's yells ceased.

He was staring over Willow's shoulder with wide eyes. She turned to see why.

Gram was holding Twig's new teddy bear in one hand and wearing a hand puppet of a fox on the other. The fox, who looked incredibly real, was sniffing the little bear. And Gram was backing the bear up as though he were trying to escape.

"Wo, wook," Twig said with one of his deep chuckles.

Thankfully, Willow loosened her iron hold and Twig went scrambling up the few steps to Gram, reaching for his bear.

Uncle Hum sat down on a lower step. He wiped his face with his apron, gave a sigh and waited, with Willow, to see what would happen next.

"Oh, Twig, you've come for me at last," Gram made the bear say, in a squeaky but very clear voice.

Willow smiled. Twig took the bear and made him approach the fox, who instantly dove around Gram's body and hid himself, out of Twig's sight.

Willow looked down at her great-uncle. He still looked as though he longed to paddle Twig's bottom. But after catching his breath, he shrugged, laughed and went back to the kitchen to load the dishwasher and clean up.

Gram went into the bathroom and shooed the dogs on into her bedroom. Then she returned and used the toys to lure Twig into the bathroom and into the tub. The little boy had not bathed in a tub more than two or three times in his life. Willow was sure he would refuse to get in. But he could not resist the bright bath toys that waited to be played with. Willow sat on the toilet seat and watched him make the yellow ducks swim and dive. She showed him how to wind up the speed boat. The first time it shot through the water, he began to scramble out. Then he saw her laughing and calmed down.

Gram came and went, keeping on eye on them, discouraging any serious splashing. Then Twig was clean and looking sleepy. After all, he had spent the five-hour plane ride wide awake.

Willow put his new pajamas on. Then she led him to the bunk bed.

"No, no," he protested but he didn't mean it.

"You put these pajamas on, Willow, and lie down beside him until he drops off," Gram suggested.

Willow had been wanting to do that very thing. The sulky scowl left Twig's face as she put on the pajamas and pushed him into the lower bunk ahead of her. Gram left the room.

"Sleep, sleep, my brother, my baby," Willow sang as Angel had taught her to, when he was newborn.

> *Sleep, sleep, my brother, my own.*
> *I am your sister, your Willow, who loves you.*
> *Sleep, sleep. You are not alone.*

She stopped then. When she looked at her brother, Twig, his thumb in his mouth, was softly snoring. She slid out of the bed and crept to the door. Nobody was in the hall but her grandmother heard her.

"I'm in here, Willow," she called.

Willow went to Gram's bedroom door and hesitated.

"Come on in, honey. I have your bath ready." Gram put down a book, got up off her bed and led the way through the door which connected her room to the bathroom. "You need a soak to help you relax. I think you're as keyed-up as I am."

Willow took off her pajamas, feeling shy even though she had not been used to privacy. She lay back in the scented water until its warmth covered all of her but her face. Her mind drifted toward sleep. She felt like a mermaid who had been out of the ocean for a while and now was home again in her proper element.

Then Gram sat down on the toilet seat and fired a question at Willow that jerked her back from the edge of dreamland.

"How much can Twig hear?"

9
Willow Talks

Willow, stiff with shock, stayed very still, trying to take in the fact that Gram had guessed Twig's secret. Would she still want them if Willow admitted that she thought he could not hear anything with his left ear and not much with his right one? Nobody else seemed to have figured this out. Maisie had thought he was retarded, she knew. But Maisie had not known Twig when he was little.

"Child, don't worry so," her grandmother's quiet voice said gently. "It won't change my decision about you or my feeling for him. You are my grandchildren and you need help. But I think Twig may need extra, that's all. I'm right, aren't I? Has he always been like this?"

Chance it, Red Mouse urged. You need her and I am sure you can trust her.

Willow cleared her throat and forced herself to speak,

even though it was hard to get the words past the lump that was choking her.

"No. I don't think so. Angel was . . . You know she takes . . . "

"She's a drug addict. Yes, I do know that. At first, I thought he was different simply because he was born addicted. But my nurse's training and years of experience have made me observant, I suppose. I soon noticed you were making sure you spoke right to him and raised your voice."

Feeling trapped in the bathtub, Willow picked up the washcloth and draped it over her face. She had to think. She must not tell everything. Surely Gram could not see all the hard memories she had hidden inside.

"I'm sorry," she heard Gram say. "You finish your bath. I should have waited. Take your time. We can talk after you're done. Would you like me to wash your hair?"

Willow lowered the washcloth, opened her mouth and then shut it again. She could not remember anyone but herself washing her hair. But it didn't need washing. It was clean enough from the shower at Star's.

"No, thank you," she said, not explaining her reasons but starting to scrub herself. Then she scrambled over the high side and found her grandmother waiting with the thick yellow towel, which seemed almost as big as a blanket. Dry and dressed in her pajamas, Willow padded after her into the bedroom next door.

"Here's something to keep you warm," Gram said, wrapping a rainbow-hued afghan loosely around her. "Now curl up in the rocker and tell me. We don't want to wake Twig."

"He won't wake up no matter how noisy I am, not when he's just gone to sleep," Willow said.

She felt sick with fear. No matter how kind her grandmother sounded, Twig was his sister's responsibility, not Gram's. What if their grandmother insisted that Twig be sent away somewhere? Nobody must separate them. Well, she'd worry about it later. If absolutely necessary, the two of them could run away again.

She remembered their time in the park and shivered. She did not want to have to run.

Gram settled herself on the bed and faced Willow. She turned on a light so they could see each other clearly. Her smile was warm but her eyes, behind their glasses, looked troubled.

"Tell me from the beginning, Willow," she said then. "And don't be frightened and leave things out. We can work together better if I know the whole truth."

Willow felt small and alone. She shivered again. She did not know where to start. She sat mute and miserable, unable to do what Gram had asked.

"Where was he born?" Gram prompted. "What was he like as a baby? Was Angel able to look after him at first?"

"He was born at Lou's place," Willow said, forcing out the words. "When Mum found out she was pregnant, she said she would stop taking drugs but the doctor said she mustn't or she'd kill the baby. But she shouldn't take any more cocaine and . . . and . . . "

"I'm sure she would have tried," Gram said huskily. "It can't have been easy."

"No," Willow said, shaking even harder as she remembered

that bad time. "You see, Julius was Twig's dad and he left when he knew she was having a baby. I really liked Julius but he didn't want to be a dad, I guess. He said he was going out to get a video and some beer but he never came back. So Angel really needed the stuff. She always does when she's unhappy. Anyway, she said she was scared to stop."

Willow's voice trailed off. Would Gram believe that? She herself had not known whether Angel was telling the truth. Lou had not believed her.

And Twig had been hurt just the same.

Her grandmother picked up a pajama top that looked as though it must belong to Uncle Hum. Two buttons were missing. She began threading a needle and then poked through a button drawer looking for one that matched. She didn't glance at Willow. The silence between them lengthened. Finally Willow gulped and plunged on.

"He was born at Lou's. Mum . . . She likes me to call her Angel . . . but she's my mother . . . she got a guy to take us up there. We'd been there a couple of days when her pains started. There wasn't time to go for a doctor. Jo and Lou live way out in this wild place in a cabin. It's really just one big room so I saw him get born."

Gram did look up at that. Her eyes were startled, shocked even. Then their expression changed to one Willow could not interpret. When she spoke, Willow heard unmistakeable envy in her voice.

"I've never seen a baby born. It must have been terrifying for you but exciting too. Was it exciting?"

Willow nodded, remembering her desperate fear and then the miracle of Twig's head pushing its way out. Lou had cut the cord and passed him, yelling and messy, to Willow.

"He's all yours," she had said, panic in her voice. "I have to get this bleeding stopped. Jo, help me."

From the moment Willow had held the small, slippery, naked baby boy, he had been hers. Before she even had him washed and wrapped in a towel, her mother had fallen into an exhausted sleep. Jo and Lou had collapsed too, grey with weariness and strain.

"Mum bled," she forged on. "So I took the baby and cleaned him off and wrapped him up in a blanket. He screamed and screamed. Then Lou gave him something to make him sleep."

"I'm sure he needed it, poor mite," Gram said. "Withdrawal is bad enough when you understand what's going on, but he must have suffered without knowing a thing."

Willow nodded.

"Lou gave him a bit of the stuff whenever we fed him but she kept making it less. Angel had had a friend whose baby was in the hospital and that's what they did there. You can't make a baby stop cold turkey. He was healthy in every other way. But Angel couldn't stand his screaming. So she said she'd go and find Julius and get help. I guessed she wouldn't be back. Lou knew too. She tried to stop her. But one morning, we woke up and she'd gone. Lou figured she arranged for the guy that brought us to come back and get her and she walked out to the road so we wouldn't hear the truck."

"Your mother may be foolish in some ways, but she's plenty smart in others," Gram said dryly, snapping off her thread.

"Yeah."

Willow thought she'd said a lot. Maybe she could say she was too tired to go on and leave the rest until another time.

Get it over with, kid, Red Mouse advised. You can do it.

Willow sighed and obeyed.

"Well, I looked after Twig as much as I could from the beginning. He was my brother and I knew they didn't really want him. Nobody wanted him . . . but me."

She added the last two words in a voice so low Gram had to strain to catch them. She put down the mending and turned to face her. Then, when her granddaughter did not say anything more, she reached out and patted the fists Willow had tightly clenched in her lap.

"What a lot to ask of a little girl," she said gently. "I can't think how you managed. Was he deaf then?"

Willow thought back to the baby Twig had been. He had loved it when anyone sang to him.

"No. He heard everything. It happened when he wasn't quite two," she said, in such a low voice her grandmother had to lean forward to catch the halting words. .

"What happened, Willow?"

"Lou's brother, Jake . . . he came. I think he was hiding out from the police or something. Lou was scared of him. So was I. Jake got really mad at Twig for screaming . . . and he . . . he kept hitting him. Lou wasn't there. He didn't listen to me. He hit Twig until he knocked him out. Jake took off when he couldn't bring Twig around."

"Oh, Willow," Gram whispered, tears in her eyes.

Willow gulped and plunged on.

"Twig came out of it but, after that, he couldn't hear me properly. Lou saw the bruises as soon as they came in and she was mad. When Jake showed up again a few months later, she never left us alone with him. After a couple of days, she got us up before sunrise, while he was asleep. She had our stuff packed. She and Jo drove us all the way back to Vancouver and tracked Angel down and made her take us back."

She took a deep breath and gabbled out the rest, wanting to get it over with.

"The two of us stayed with her for quite a while. We moved from one place to another. Angel has lots of friends. Then, near the end, she left us with Maisie. I guess you heard what happened from Ms Thornton."

Willow could not understand why she felt so ashamed. She could not have made Jake stop beating up Twig, could she? If she had come between them, it might have been worse.

But she had not tried to come between them. That was the part that made her feel so hateful still. Twig had been screaming and Jake had shoved her out of the way and gone for him. She had gone sprawling halfway across the room and had crawled under the table and crouched there. She had not gone to Twig until the man had slammed out of the cabin door and roared away in his truck.

Twig had come to half an hour later but he had lain still, whimpering, and had not seemed to hear her. When Lou and Jo returned from their trip to the store, forty kilometres away, she had tried to make them take Twig to a doctor. But Lou said the nearest doctor was too far from the cabin.

One of the women should have stayed with them, she thought, but the trip for supplies was part of their routine and Jake had not hurt them before. He had always frightened her though, and she knew his sister feared him. Otherwise she would have kicked him out.

Remembering, Willow's face burned and she could not look up at Gram. After all, she had heard Twig scream her name and had stayed frozen where she was.

"You have been a brave girl, Willow Wind Jones," Gram said. "Whatever happened, it was not your fault. Never forget that. You have taken care of Twig when lots of sisters would have given up. He's here now and he's safe all because of you."

Willow blinked. Her eyes felt hot. She wanted to believe the words but she couldn't. She remembered too vividly how she had hidden under that table until Jake had gone. She remembered, with a lurch of nausea, smiling at him, trying to make him like her. Later, she had smiled at Rae too. She was a coward and she knew it.

Gram did not know, not yet.

"Has Twig seen a doctor?"

Gram let the quiet question hang in the air between them. Willow's silence told her the answer. She stood up abruptly.

"Bed for you, my child," she said. "We'll waken you at lunchtime or you won't sleep tonight. Come on. I'll sing you a song I sang to your mother. We'll think about what to do for Twig later."

As soon as Willow was tucked into her bunk and Gram began to sing quietly, Willow knew she had heard the song before. Angel's voice seemed to sing along with Gram's. In spite of her worries, Willow fell asleep like someone toppling off a cliff and tumbling down, down into darkness. The last thing she heard was Gram singing.

10
Crocus

She woke an hour later without being called. Twig still slept deeply, his arms thrown wide, his hoarse breathing going steadily on.

"I'll be back," his sister whispered to him.

She put on the clean clothes Gram had left on the chair. Then she went to the top of the stairs and listened. The two tiny dogs with ears like wings danced into the hall below, glanced up at her, yipped a greeting and chased each other down the hall and out of sight. She heard the slap-flap of the dog doors. A big bark from far away told her that Sirius was outside. She could detect no sound that related to humans.

She slipped down the carpeted stairs, pulling on the fleecy, hooded sweatshirt she had found in her room, and eased open the door to the front porch. Then, shutting it behind her, she crossed and opened the door to the outside world.

A scrawny orange tabby cat sat on the step and looked up at her.

"Meeouw," it said.

Willow crouched down and held out her fingers for the cat to sniff. He seemed to like her smell. He poked her hand with his triangular nose and then licked her right thumb thoroughly with his sandpaper tongue.

"Hello, cat," she whispered. "Are you the stray they don't want?"

The cat gave another conversational mew. He rubbed the side of his head even harder against her knuckles. Then he rose and stalked across the grass.

"Come on," he seemed to be telling her.

Willow grinned.

"I shouldn't leave Twig," she said.

The cat thought this was foolishness. He gave her a scornful glance. He appeared to think Twig could manage without her fussing over him. Cats, on the other hand, deserved complete attention from their human slaves.

Go, Red Mouse said. It's time.

Willow straightened up and looked around. Since leaving Gram's, except for the years she had spent at Jo and Lou's, she had never been outside a city. Even there, she had not been able to see far for the crowding bush. She had also been wary of the wild animals they glimpsed crossing the clearing. Bears, elk, moose.

Here, what seemed like miles of open land stretched down a hill to a stream. At least, she thought it was a stream. It was too far away to be certain. The still-wintry wind bit through her downy sweatshirt as though it were made of thin cotton.

Something butted against her ankle.

Willow knew it had to be the stray cat but she had just seen one splash of the same orange in the half-frozen garden. The cat's coat was that exact shade of flame yellow. She went and knelt to see better. It was a flower and it was one she thought she knew. A crocus. She'd seen them in Vancouver gardens. There was a clump here but only one had actually opened its hopeful petals.

The cat had followed her. He wove around her, rubbing himself against her warmth, and purring. The purr was rough. He had not been using it much.

"Okay, Crocus," she said softly, rubbing his neat head with its velvety ears. She flattened them with her hand and they felt limp but the moment her hand moved away, up they flicked, listening, alert.

Crocus was a perfect name, she decided. He was a stray and tough, like the flowers blooming despite the wintry weather. And the sounds he made were croaky. He wasn't very big. He must be young.

The door opened and Gram looked out.

"Don't tell me that cat is still sticking around," she said, coming over. "We have four dogs, puss. We also have Twig, who might not take kindly to being scratched. Maybe I should take you in to the Humane Society."

Willow did not need to ask what the Humane Society was, even though, in Vancouver, it was called the SPCA. She bent and let her hand run down the cat's body again from head to tail.

"His name is Crocus," she said without looking up.

"Oh, Willow, don't tell me you've named him," Gram

moaned. "It's much harder to hand over an animal once you've named it. But you can see for yourself that no cat in his right mind would want to move in here."

"He might," Willow said stubbornly, not joining in her grandmother's laughter. "We could let him decide. I'm sure he's hungry. I can feel all his bones. And he's tough. Twig likes cats."

"You'll find tinned dog food on top of the fridge," Gram said. "No, you stay here. I'll get it. He might run off if you left."

Willow grinned at the sudden about-face. While she waited for Gram to return, she went on petting Crocus and taking in more of Stonecrop's surroundings. She noted the paved driveway that circled round a large tree. There was a big garage. It looked as though it could hold three cars. The yard seemed almost as big as Stanley Park. And there was an old willow tree, its long bare branches swaying in the March wind.

"Here you go, Crocus," Gram said, coming out with a dog dish in her hand.

Crocus went at it as though he had not eaten for weeks. Both Willow and her grandmother watched him gulping and swallowing the food at top speed. Halfway through, he seemed to become aware of their watching eyes, for he slowed down slightly and showed more decorum.

"He's not quite as starved as he appears," Gram said. "I put some scraps out last night and not only was the dish empty this morning but there were two partially eaten mice left as a token of his appreciation. I must say I would like help with the mice. The brazen little beasts have been eating us out of house and home. I caught one right up on the kitchen counter yesterday and he practically thumbed his nose at me before he shot off."

Willow thought of Red Mouse and grinned. Thank goodness Crocus could never do him in. She wondered if she should feel sorry for the real mice. She did feel slightly sad about them, but she loved Crocus already.

"We could hang a bell around his neck," she offered.

"I doubt it would stay there for long," Gram said. "And what if it warned the mice away?"

The front door opened and Uncle Hum stuck his head out.

"Nell!" he called. "Willow! Are you two out here? Twig is awake."

Willow heard him yelling and ran for the house.

"Wait, Hum," she heard Gram say as she flew by, "how do you like the name Crocus for a cat?"

"You haven't gone and named him," Uncle Hum said. "As if we haven't enough on our plates . . . "

Willow grinned again as she pounded up the stairs. Uncle Hum might be older but she knew already that her grandmother almost always got her way. Maybe Uncle Hum gave in to her because she was younger. Twig got his own way too.

She could hardly wait to show him Crocus. The cat was so alive. Once Twig saw him, the ghost of the black kitten might no longer haunt him.

He had stopped crying by the time she reached the bedroom door. He was doing his best to haul Tiggy up onto his bunk. She was choking until Willow dived to her rescue. Freed from his grip, the Scottie gave Twig's hand a quick lick and wagged her tail. Then she jumped down and trundled out the door.

"You shouldn't do that," Willow said, feeling helpless. She got Twig into his clothes. Now what? She had no idea how to keep him busy here. First she might take him to meet Crocus. She clutched his hand and half-led, half-dragged him to the top of the stairs. Then he jerked his hand away and, before she guessed what he was about to do, he straddled the banister and went whizzing to the bottom.

"Twig!" Willow gasped, her eyes wide.

"Try it yourself," Gram said. "It's a child-tested banister. It's been in use for over a hundred years."

While Willow stood and stared down at her, Twig bounced back up the long flight, jumped onto the banister and was flying down it again. Willow moved fast this time. As soon as he was out of the way, she was sliding down herself. It was fun. She felt as though she had wings, as though she was a kid with no worries, as though she could handle anything. In spite of herself, she shrieked with delight.

Then, suddenly, Twig had had enough. As he slid to the floor and looked around for trouble to get into, Willow sped to him, grabbed his hand and yanked him out the door. If only Crocus was still there . . .

He was. He meowed a greeting and came toward Willow, rubbing against their legs. She was tense, ready to grab Twig's hands away if he hurt the cat. But he did not. He squatted down, held out his hand and waited. Crocus bumped his head against the small fingers. The little boy looked up at his sister with wide, wondering eyes.

"Wo, ca', ca'!" he shouted.

Willow remembered the dead kitten. She smiled at her excited little brother and nodded.

"Crocus," she said loudly into his hearing ear. "Crocus."

"Cokes," said Twig. "Goo' ca', Goo' Cokes."

Crocus slanted an ear back, rubbed against Twig and began to purr. Twig, feeling this, was astonished. He chuckled. It was Angel's throaty chuckle exactly.

11
Aunt Con

Twig's pleasure at seeing Crocus was a bright moment in a day filled with tension. Willow could not persuade her brother to leave the dogs alone and, when Crocus was lured in, Twig chased the cat as well. Crocus wanted a home badly, though.

"Maybe that cat will move on," Uncle Hum said, as Crocus streaked past with Twig flying after him.

But even though Crocus fled under beds and scaled dressers to elude Twig's reaching hands, he did not try to escape through the dog door.

"Does this boy ever get calmer?" Gram inquired, mopping her forehead.

"Sometimes," Willow answered cautiously, not wanting to raise their hopes too high. Twig did sleep, after all. He was very calm when he was fast asleep. And while watching TV at Star's, he had seemed mesmerized. Willow hoped there was television here. It would certainly help.

Twig did finally settle down when he discovered the colour TV in the den. He sat entranced, watching "Sesame Street" and "The Polka Dot Door." The fact that he could not hear what the characters were saying did not seem to bother him. He looked as happy as a clam as he watched the antics of Big Bird and Barney. He clearly liked animated bits or puppets best. He still shifted his body about, banged his feet up and down, slid off the couch and climbed back on over and over again. But, while his body moved, his eyes remained fixed on the screen.

Watching him, Willow felt relief and apprehension. Wait until they wanted him to come away from the TV. She knew, with a sinking heart, that it would be extremely difficult to move him on to the next activity without his making a scene.

Sufficient unto the day is the worry thereof, Red Mouse remarked, sounding like Gram this time.

When Gram was busy getting supper, though, Uncle Hum somehow managed to entice Twig out for a walk with himself and Sirius. Willow perched on a kitchen stool watching her grandmother stirring something on the stove. Whatever it was, it smelled delicious. She gave a contented sigh.

Then the phone rang.

"Would you get that, please, Willow?" Gram said over her shoulder. "I'll be free in a minute but I can't leave this until it's thickened."

Willow reached for the receiver hanging on the wall. Her hand trembled slightly. She had hardly ever spoken on a phone. She could not remember ever being asked to answer one before.

"Hello," she said.

"Oh, bother. I must have the wrong number," a woman snapped. She hung up with a bang that hurt Willow's ear. Willow stared at the receiver. Then, slowly, she reached out and replaced it.

Gram turned from the stove.

"What on earth . . . ?" she began.

The phone shrilled again. Willow stepped back and put her hands behind her.

"I'll get it," her grandmother said. "Hello . . . Oh, Con, it's you. Where are you?"

She stood listening for a moment. Willow was near enough to be quite sure it was the same sharp-voiced, rude woman. Her heart sank.

"Got the wrong number, did you say? . . . Some brat answered . . . Well, it must have been the wrong number then. We certainly have no brats here . . . "

She listened again, flashing a grin at Willow as she did so.

"All right. We'll be expecting you tomorrow then. Say hi to Leslie and Danielle for me. What's been going on here? Nothing that can't wait until tomorrow morning. I'm in the middle of getting supper. See you."

She hung up ever so gently. Then she made a rude face at the phone.

"That was my dear sister," she said needlessly. "She'll be back tomorrow morning. I can't wait."

Her expression made Willow uncomfortable.

"Why didn't you tell her about us?" she asked, avoiding looking into Gram's too observant eyes.

"I wanted to keep you for a surprise," Gram said, removing the pot from the stove.

Neither of them spoke for a few minutes. Gram got salad stuff out of the fridge, rinsed it off and began to chop it up. At last she sighed and, letting the vegetables wait, turned to face Willow.

"I had better do my best to prepare you for the scene that will take place when Constance arrives and meets my 'brats,'" she said, leaning back against the counter. "I don't want you to be hurt. You deserve fair warning, even if she doesn't. Wait till we've eaten though."

She did not talk about Aunt Con again until Twig was settled for the night and Uncle Hum had gone downstairs with his Talking Book. Then Gram picked up the mending she had been working on earlier and filled Willow in. She kept her eyes on the torn sleeve she was repairing and seemed preoccupied by it.

"First, you should know that this house belongs to Hum and me. Con sold out her share to us and so really has no say in what we do here. We could set up an orphanage for fifty infants or decide to raise chinchillas in the attic and it would be none of Con's business. She was not invited to move in with us. She has a condominium in London and seemed comfortably ensconced there and Hum and I were happily living our lives on the old family farm, which belonged, free and clear, to the two of us."

She stopped talking long enough to thread another needle. Willow bided her time.

"Then, right after Christmas, she descended upon us, bag and baggage."

Willow's heart sank.

"You mean she came for a visit?" she asked, keeping her face as blank as she could and her tone of voice careful. After all, these women were sisters. She knew how mad she felt when people made remarks about Twig.

"Well, that's what we thought. Constance herself hasn't said. She says she's been told she has Chronic Fatigue Syndrome and should rest and so she came home to do it in the bosom of her family. That was three months ago and she shows no signs of leaving. Hum and I keep hinting. But it's tricky. She's the oldest, you see, and she's considered herself the boss since we were babies."

Willow's startled eyes lifted involuntarily to Gram's face.

"But you aren't babies now," she said. "You were married! You're old . . . "

Gram's laugh had a grim note.

"You're right—although I have known babies who were married. Con isn't in charge, hasn't been for years, but it's hard to change family patterns, Willow. We are driven crazy by her. But we do feel sorry for her. Hum and I are kindred spirits, you see, and she's the odd man out. We don't laugh at the same things . . . It's hard to explain."

"She won't like us, will she?" Willow asked, going straight to the point.

"I am quite sure she will not like you one little bit. I think she's going to be thoroughly unpleasant about you and Twig joining us. It's none of her business but . . . it's the way she is. So you have to be warned. You'll have to be polite to her, Willow, but otherwise don't let her get under your skin."

"Is she . . . really awful?" Willow half-whispered.

"Sometimes. Never, ever, listen to her when she talks about your being a burden. She will. Oh, dear. Thank God for Hum. He keeps me from flying off the handle every hour on the hour."

"She'll hate Twig," Willow said. It was not a question and Gram did not treat it as one.

"Yes, she will hate Twig," she agreed. "She had a soft spot for Star but she never cared for your mother. When you were here as a baby, she was so disgusted with me for helping Angel out that she didn't darken the door for a couple of years. It was very restful."

Willow laughed in spite of herself. After a moment, her grandmother laughed too, but wearily.

"When Angel took me away, did she come back? What did she say?"

"You shouldn't ask and I suppose I shouldn't tell you. She came to see me a couple of days after you'd gone, when I was missing you terribly. And my sister told me to thank my lucky stars I wasn't being landed with you for life. 'When that girl comes whining back,' she said, 'don't let her in the door or you'll never get rid of her.' Hum told her to leave and I didn't speak to her for weeks."

"I wouldn't have come here after that," Willow said.

"Ah, but you're not Con. She's like a bulldozer or a tank. She doesn't notice that she's knocking you down and squashing you flat. She thinks she's telling you things you need to know. And eventually you just give up trying to change her."

Willow had known people like that. She steered clear of them and kept Twig away too whenever she could.

Gram had stopped pretending to sew. She sighed.

"I'm afraid she'll be as nasty as she can when she finds you're here again. Poor Con. It's herself she hurts really. Be strong and of good courage, Willow. This, too, shall pass."

In bed that night, Willow went over the surprising conversation, doing her best to get ready for this great-aunt who sounded like a monster. But she could not plan a strategy ahead of time, not until she saw where the attack was going to come from.

The next day, Gram sent Willow out to bring in the mail. Willow pulled on her new anorak and a pair of warm red mittens Gram had found for her, and went down the drive to the mailbox. Already she knew she was going to love this small job. She needed to get out of the house. Just feeling the wind blowing against her face and seeing it tumbling the masses of cloud out of its way to reveal splashes of blue made her feel enormously free.

She still did not know for certain if she and Twig would be allowed to stay for good but she was growing convinced that Gram would fight to keep them. Uncle Hum liked them too . . . most of the time. Aunt Con was an unknown quantity though.

Willow was lifting the flap on the metal mailbox when a car pulled up behind her with a squeal of brakes.

"Just what do you think you're doing?" said the sharp voice she had heard over the phone the day before.

Willow froze for a moment. She stared at the woman in the car like a rabbit staring at a snake. Aunt Con had large dark glasses on and lots of make-up and blonde hair. Blonde! Hadn't Gram said she was the eldest? And her plum-coloured mouth was twisted in an ugly sneer.

"Answer me. And put back anything you've already taken from the box. Nothing there has anything to do with you. I ought to turn you over to the police."

Willow stiffened her spine and deliberately reached in for the mail Gram had sent her to fetch. Aunt Con might be the boss of her brother and sister, but Willow Wind Jones was not going to let herself be pushed around.

"I am Willow Jones and my grandmother asked me to get these letters," she said as coolly as she could manage. "I'm doing what I was told."

"Your grandmother!" Aunt Con's voice rose to a shriek that made Willow want to cover her ears. "What on earth do you mean?"

Willow didn't answer. Clutching the mail against her chest, she ducked around the car and raced up the lane to the big stone house which had looked bleak at first but which now looked as though it were waiting for her.

The door opened as she reached it. Gram pulled her inside.

"I'm sorry," she said under her breath, looking past her granddaughter at the car speeding up the drive. "Of all the bad luck! Con was always good at appearing just when she wasn't wanted."

Aunt Con shot out of her car as though she had springs in her shoes. She slammed the door so hard Willow flinched. She had removed her dark glasses and was glaring at her sister and great-niece with steely blue eyes. She stormed up the walk, talking as she came.

"What on earth has been going on here while my back was turned? Who is this child? Angel's brat, I assume. Why is she here? Hasn't that girl given you enough trouble without shipping her unwanted offspring here? Well, I won't let her get away with it this time. I'll make sure and certain she gets the message that we are through with her once and for all. Who does she think she is?"

"Angel knows who she is. She's my daughter and Willow is my granddaughter and she was invited to come," Gram said. Her voice was soft but deadly.

Willow stared at her in awe. Gram went on, every word clear as glass. "She's going to be making her home here. Not only she but . . . "

Twig, like his great-aunt, had a way of arriving just when he was not wanted. He picked that moment to catapult through the hall, chasing Aunt Con's two tiny dogs and screaming with laughter as they dashed away.

"Stop that child!" screeched Aunt Con, making even more noise than her great-nephew. "Who in the name of all that's holy is he?"

The dogs raced to hide behind her as Gram did her best to make the introduction.

"Twig! Only Angel would give a child such an outlandish name. You never said she'd had another one?"

Gram just looked at her sister. She did not admit she had never heard of Twig until the day before he arrived. Aunt Con's face was very red and her breathing huffed and puffed alarmingly. She looked at Twig, now struggling to free himself from his sister's grip, as though he'd just crawled out from under a rock.

"Well, go and pack their bags, Nell. I mean it. I can't be expected to live with hooligans like that. I need peace and quiet. I told you what my doctor—"

"In that case," said a deep voice from behind Gram, "it's your bags we'll be packing, Constance. Because peace is over and done with and quiet is a thing of the past in this house. War has been declared. No more settling into being Senior Citizens. Nell and I are starting our youth over."

Aunt Con opened her mouth to yell at Uncle Hum.

Then Crocus stepped forward, meowed loudly and rubbed against her ankles.

Gram began to laugh helplessly. Aunt Con stared at her in outrage. Uncle Hum smiled. The bedlam grew worse. Aunt Con's arrival and Twig's dash after the small dogs had all the dogs barking their heads off by now.

Willow looked up into her great-aunt's stricken face and was startled. She saw fear looking back at her, panic, terror even. She knew fear. She knew how it felt to lose the only home you had. She did not like this woman but still, coming home to two unknown children plus a cat must have been a shock.

The understatement of the year, Red Mouse murmured. Help her.

Willow choked down a giggle and took a moment to extract a letter from those in her hand.

"There's a letter for you, Aunt," she said. Then she did her best to smile. "Twig's not as bad as he looks. He's just not settled in yet. Beat it, Crocus."

She shoved the cat away from the woman's ankles with her foot and turned to the adults for help.

"All right, Willow," Gram said as though her granddaughter had told her to behave. "For pity's sake, come on in, Con. I just made a fresh pot of coffee. Hum, take the mail so

Willow can hold onto her brother with both hands. Then we'll have lunch before we say something we'll all regret."

Aunt Con surprised everyone by leaning on Willow's shoulder as she stepped into the front hall with a sigh of pure relief. Willow realized Aunt Con had actually thought, for a second, that they were going to evict her.

"Well, well, you are quite a girl, niece," said Uncle Hum so softly that only she caught the words. "You'll bear watching. You're too perceptive for someone so young."

Willow turned her back on him. She still found it unsettling to hear Red Mouse's voice coming from somebody else's mouth. She would think about what he had said later. Now she had Twig to calm down and that took all her strength and cunning.

12
Beginnings

Aunt Con ate her lunch in a deafening silence. Willow had never heard someone make so much noise without saying a word. Her great-aunt sighed gustily, banged her elbow down on the table, chewed and swallowed so that they could hear every bite going down, made her fork clatter and her plastic tumbler knock into the salt shaker.

Every time Willow stole a glance at her, she seemed to be staring back. The moment she caught Willow's eye, Aunt Con would shake her head or roll her eyes.

This made Willow uncomfortable, but it delighted Twig. He hooted with laughter and shook his head. Then he looked at his sister and, whenever he knew she was watching, he would twist his own face in imitation of this strange new person. He blew his lips out, too, and wiped non-existent sweat from his brow. Then he pointed his finger at Aunt Con and rolled his eyes up so high they almost completely disappeared. He sent his sister into a splutter of giggles.

"Excuse me," she gasped and, with her face scarlet, grabbed Twig and dragged him from the kitchen.

"Brats! What on earth were you thinking of?" she heard Aunt Con start in.

From then on, for an hour or more, Willow could hear the woman's harsh voice badgering Gram and Uncle Hum about deciding to take the children in without so much as phoning her.

"You didn't leave us a number," Gram said in a voice so cold she might have been keeping it in the freezer. "But even if you had, we would have had no need to inform you, Constance. This is not your house, remember. You are not the hostess here; you are a guest. An uninvited guest, I might add."

Twig had returned to the helpful TV, so Willow was free to slip back to the battlefield. She stayed near the door, where Gram could see her but Aunt Con could not.

Aunt Con pretended not to have heard the last bit. She sailed on, piling up arguments. Gram and Uncle Hum were far too old to raise children. They knew nothing about Willow and Twig's culture. They didn't know about the children's health either.

"They could have AIDS or TB—anything."

"All the more reason to take them," Uncle Hum said when Gram took a moment drawing a long breath. "We didn't ask you for a health certificate."

Aunt Con glared at him and swept on. There wasn't room in the house for two more inhabitants. She gave that argument up fast when she realized that Gram was going to agree and add that they needed her room.

"The boy is clearly incorrigible. Face facts. Did you see how he went for Toby and Panda? If he had been allowed, he would have injured or even killed them. They are delicate. A rare breed."

With Twig in the house, she insisted, none of them would have an easy moment. Why, he could drown the tiny dogs or break their legs when nobody was looking.

"He'd have to catch them first," Uncle Hum said. "I've had enough of this. I'm going downstairs. If you need me, Nell, holler."

"Deserter," Gram murmured, but he pretended not to hear.

At last, Aunt Con agreed to stop talking about it for the rest of the day. "On condition you and Humphrey do some thinking!" she put in.

"We have a cat to settle in as well as two children," Gram said firmly. "And I've done my thinking already. Willow, you and Twig come into the den and help me catch Crocus. We'll have to get him to a vet or he may pass on parasites. Also we'll have him neutered. There are enough toms prowling these parts."

Helping to corral the cat was harder than it sounded. Twig did it finally by simply grabbing his tail and holding on even though Crocus squirmed and scratched. Twig did not want Gram to take the animal and pop him into one of the dog crates she had ready but was persuaded by a deep scratch. Both children went along to the vet's office.

"I knew you collected dogs, Nell," the woman said, looking into Crocus's ears. "But I didn't know you were picking up cats and children too."

"Well, Louise, you know now. I'm a good picker, aren't I?" Gram said pleasantly. She was holding Crocus tightly and she had instructed Willow to keep a grip on Twig. There was no real need though. He was wide-eyed from the moment they entered the waiting room and came face to face with a Saint Bernard.

They left Crocus to be neutered and went shopping at the supermarket. Twig rode in the cart. That, too, was a new experience for him, and as long as Gram managed to keep far enough from the piles of food to prevent his snatching things off the shelves, they got along fine. Willow fetched the items her grandmother pointed to.

"A couple of books I ordered are in," Gram said once the grocery bags were safely in the van. "Do you want to come into The Bookshelf with me or wait in the car?"

"I don't care," Willow said.

"Willow, what are you thinking?" Gram said.

Willow hesitated.

"It would be easier to stay out here with Twig, I know," she said finally, not looking at her grandmother, "but . . . I've never been in a bookstore."

Gram stared at her for a moment. Then she laughed softly.

"You have, you know," she said. "You've even been in this very one. I took you myself when you were little. I remember buying you *The Story about Ping* and *Madeline*. But you must come now, of course, and so must Twig. We'll have to get a good grip on him though."

They all went in. Gram picked up a couple of new mysteries. Willow peered at each, wondering what they were about. Then Gram led them both to the children's section.

"You choose one each for yourselves," she said, "and I'll get you a couple I know you'll like."

Willow wanted to linger over choosing but she didn't dare. Twig snatched up two board books, one about trains and one about dinosaurs.

"Good thinking, Twig," Gram said. "He's old enough to take care of books but I think he still needs ones that can take some rough handling. Let's get some with great pictures."

"You said one," Willow reminded her shyly as her grandmother added three more to Twig's pile.

"Books are like food," she said. "You can't live without them. I think you two have been on a starvation diet. You can take more than one too."

Willow chose fast. She looked up and saw Gram smiling.

"Those are all good," her grandmother said.

"How do you know?"

"I've read them, of course. I read that one about Gilly Hopkins to your mother. And remember that your Uncle Hum writes for children."

Willow was astonished to find herself the owner of three brand new books. Gram caught her amazement and laughed, then turned to Twig.

"Whoops! No, Twig. Not quite that many."

Willow took the towering stack out of Twig's clutch, handed them to Gram and grabbed his hand.

"We'll wait outside," she said and pulled him along out onto the street. He scowled and dragged his feet but, since he liked being outside better than being in, he soon began pointing at vehicles which he thought wonderful: a city bus, a truck with a German shepherd looking out the cab window, an elderly car painted hot pink.

They were nearly home when Gram pulled the van off the road and parked in front of a school. "I'm going in to fill out some forms about you," she said to Willow. "I phoned. They said you could start this coming Monday."

"Start . . . " Willow said blankly.

"School," Gram said. "Do you want to bring Twig in or shall I bring the principal out to meet you?"

"I'll stay here," Willow mumbled. She almost yelled that she did not want to go to school but it would not be true. She'd wanted to go ever since she was six.

The man who followed Gram out a few minutes later was friendly. His eyes were kind. Willow waited for him to be shocked out of his mind when he found out she had never attended school like other kids. But he remained calm.

"I'll see you Monday morning bright and early," he said, stepping away from the van. "We'll sort out what grade you belong in then."

When they pulled away, Willow did not speak. She couldn't. But Twig made up for her silence as he pointed out a tall man on a tall horse and a fox standing in a field, staring at them.

The moment they arrived home, Twig became mesmerized by "Sesame Street" again. The big colour TV was still a miracle to him and a relief to his worried sister.

"Well, how much did that trip cost you?" Aunt Con said nastily, eyeing the bulging bag Willow had carried in.

"I guess there's no such thing as a free cat," Gram said with a laugh. "She thinks Crocus is only about five months old. Somebody must have had trouble finding a home for kittens and dropped him off in the country."

"Strays are always expensive," Aunt Con said, staring at Willow.

Willow knew she was not really talking about Crocus. She knew that they could be called strays. Twig and she had cost their grandmother far more than Crocus. Plane tickets to start with and long-distance phone calls and new clothes and extra food and now books. But Gram never seemed to mind.

"My best-loved pets have all been strays," Gram said.

Willow heard but was too busy thinking to feel grateful. Twig, not the money, was her biggest worry. Aunt Con sure was going to hate it when he had a screaming fit. Well, nobody liked it. Even Twig acted afraid of himself at times. Yet, in spite of the fear, he seemed unable to stop without Willow holding onto him tightly and pinning him down on a bed or a couch until he was worn out. Reason did not work with Calypso Jones.

Calypso! That was Twig's real name. Gram had asked two or three times what his name was. Willow knew she could not go on pretending not to have heard. Soon, she would have to tell.

But Calypso was a terrible name for Twig. He could not hear. Maybe Julius could have held him tight and sung "Day-O" and made him understand. But Julius had not stuck around long enough to teach his son. Julius was not a stayer.

What would Twig do when she had to leave for school?

"Would you like to take Tiggy for a walk, Willow?" Gram asked. "She loves getting out and I so seldom take her. She has the run of the fenced-in yard out back but she loves a stroll up and down the drive."

Willow was only too happy to go. She snapped on Tiggy's leash and led the wildly excited Scottie out the front door and along the lane. She looked out down the stretch of hillside which widened into a sweep of valley. Never before had she seen such a view. Oh, there had been the mountains and the sea, but she had not been free to stand gazing at them. And the land near Lou's cabin had had a wild beauty too, but she had been afraid there. She had always had to be wary of wild animals prowling. Here nothing could sneak up on you. Here you could simply stand and let the land smooth out all the hurt, rough, sore places inside you.

A robin flew into one of the trees on her other side and chirped a greeting.

Tiggy looked up and barked once. It sounded as though she and the bird were old friends.

I wonder if I'll make friends here, Willow thought wistfully. She doubted it. She had never had a friend her own age.

They reached the road and Willow turned.

A crooked rail fence ran across the front of the property. Leaning on it was a girl in a blue padded jacket and a knitted cap.

Willow stood still and waited for her to yell something mean. She got ready to say that she had a right to be here, that she belonged at Stonecrop, that it was her home. She squared her shoulders and stuck out her chin.

"Thank goodness you finally came outside on your own," the girl said, grinning. "My mother wouldn't let me go over until you had a chance to settle in. I was so excited when your grandmother came over for extra eggs and told us you were coming. Mum says I get carried away but every other kid on this road is a boy. I've been praying for a girl for years. I'm Sabrina Marr. I have twin sisters, teenagers, and a little brother who is a pain in the butt. I just turned eleven last Saturday. How old are you?"

A brief, uncertain smile tilted up the corners of Willow's mouth and vanished as swiftly as it had come. She stared at the other girl for several seconds without saying a word. Then the smile curved her lips again.

"Nobody here knows, but I'm turning eleven next Saturday," she said.

13
Sabrina Marr

"Wow!" Sabrina exclaimed, scrambling over the fence and rushing across the melting snow to fetch up next to the girl and dog. "That's cool! We're practically twins!"

Willow laughed. This girl was not like the few she had met in Vancouver. They had prowled around Willow like cats considering whether to pick a fight now or wait until later. They kept their real selves hooded. Willow did too, most of the time. It was the safest way to start. Yet it was impossible to go on being cagey or shy around Sabrina Marr. She was no cat; she was a leaping, tail-wagging puppy.

And she looked as funny as she sounded. Her eyes were almost green. Willow had never seen such greyish-green in any eyes before. They were the colour of the ocean on a cloudy day. Her cheeks and nose and even her forehead were peppered with faded freckles which must look like measles in the summer. Her reddish-brown hair stuck out in a great wild bush. Gram would have had a hard time getting her comb through such tangles. And, even though she was eleven, she had a big space between her front teeth. Her beaky nose seemed too big for her and her mouth looked as though it never quit smiling.

The two of them began following Tiggy back toward the house. Willow had a feeling she should be asking interested questions but she could not think of anything safe to ask. She didn't want Sabrina quizzing her, after all. She didn't want to have to field disturbing questions like "How long are you here for?" or "Where's your mother?"

"Mrs. Jones said you had a little brother," Sabrina said.

It wasn't a question exactly but Willow knew that she was supposed to tell the other girl something about Twig. What could she say? He was her brother and he was weird. End of discussion.

"He's four," she said finally. "He's called Twig."

"Twig? Why?" Sabrina wanted to know.

"Because I'm Willow and he's always hanging onto me, I guess," Willow mumbled. "I think that's how it got started."

"Not now, he isn't," the other girl observed.

Willow stopped walking. It was true. Twig had been watching "Sesame Street" when she had left the house but the program must be over by this time and he had not shouted, "Wo! Wo!" Where was he? Surely he was not bugging Aunt Con.

Without stopping to explain her hurry, Twig's big sister began to run toward the house. Tiggy bounded along, her tail high, her ears up and forward. Sabrina, taken off guard, soon ran after them and caught up before they reached the front door.

"What's up? Do you have to go in already?" she asked, her voice filled with disappointment.

"It's Twig," Willow tried to explain in as few words as possible. "He can be wild. I have to keep him from acting up . . . Aunt Con doesn't . . . "

"Mrs. Jones will look after him," Sabrina said casually, as though looking after Twig was nothing. "She's good with little kids."

"Yes, I know, but I have to make sure he's okay. Everything here is strange to him."

"Can't you bring him out to play for just a few minutes? I can't go inside your house. My mother told me I had to wait. But if you stayed out . . . "

Willow hesitated. Then, as if on cue, she heard Twig beginning to yell the house down. He was bellowing her name. She dashed into the front porch, without stopping to shut the door before pulling open the door into the house. As though they had been lying in wait, knowing she would do that very thing, Toby and Panda flew past her and scampered out into the snowy yard. Before she could turn to chase them, a frantic four-year-old flung himself upon her as though he had been searching for her for hours instead of minutes.

"Oh, oh, my darling boys! Catch them! They'll get run over!" Aunt Con screeched.

Sabrina, her eyes blazing with delight, took after the tiny dogs, who were flying through the trees and diving under the bushes in hot pursuit of some small creature.

Twig let go of Willow and leaped up and down, sounding louder than a fire siren.

Willow wanted to clap her hands over her ears and run away to the peace and safety of the attic. Instead, remembering how she had caught Twig on occasion, she dashed down the drive, splashing through slush, until she was level with the fleeing dogs. Then she whistled as shrilly as she could manage. They stopped in their tracks, their giant ears standing straight up, their eyes gleaming. When she knew they had seen her, Willow wheeled around and ran for the house as fast as she could go. As she had hoped, the two little dogs came chasing after her, all agog to know why she was tearing along that way. Aunt Con, seeing what she was doing, had the presence of mind to pull Twig out of the doorway. Sabrina stood still and, when the papillons flew into the house at Willow's heels, she was there to slam the porch door closed behind them.

"Way to go!" Sabrina applauded from outside.

Twig, indignant at being grabbed so unceremoniously, ducked his head down to bite Aunt Con's wrist, but Willow saw his plan in time to snatch him bodily from his great-aunt's grasp.

Gram, who seemed to have seen the whole thing, came from the kitchen with a big sugar cookie for Twig. As he bit into it, the uproar stopped. Aunt Con went down on her knees to croon over the small dogs, who licked her chin and cheeks and wagged their tails enthusiastically. Willow was sure that, if she stepped over and opened the two doors once more, both dogs would instantly scoot outside again. Brief as their freedom had been, they had been jubilant during every second of it.

"You see, Con, that our Willow has her uses," Gram said mildly. "She retrieved your darlings without permitting a hair of their heads to be damaged."

Aunt Con, her face flushed and her eyes snapping, sat back on the carpet and said, "She let them out! She probably did it on purpose."

Willow gasped but Gram patted her shoulder in reassurance.

"She knows you didn't do any such thing," she said. "She's snatching at straws. Why didn't Sabrina come in with you?"

"Her mother won't let her come inside," Willow explained, her lips twitching at the sight of Sabrina's face pressed so hard against the glass pane in the outer door that the end of her nose was white and flattened.

"It will be all right if I invite her in," Gram said, going to admit Sabrina. "For pity's sake, child, come on in. I wouldn't want you to miss anything."

Sabrina's cheeks reddened a little but she bounced into the hall and beamed around at everyone collected there.

"My mum does say I'm nosy," she confessed. "But I had to come over to meet Willow. Just think! I've lived on this road for ten years without any other girl close to my age for a neighbour."

Twig, licking the last bits of sugar cookie off his top lip, pressed close to Willow and glared at Sabrina.

"He's jealous," Sabrina laughed. "Has the green-eyed monster got you? What did you say his name was?"

"He's called Twig and he doesn't understand what you're saying," Willow said, putting her arm around her small brother's stiff shoulders and patting his arm quietly. If only it worked! She felt that she couldn't bear Sabrina to see Twig go into a wild tantrum.

Uncle Hum created a diversion. He emerged through the door to the basement, Sirius at his side as always.

"Did I hear the voice of my friend Sabrina Marr?" he called, coming toward the group still standing near the front door.

"Hi-Ho, Hum," Sabrina called back, her face lighting up. She hurried to meet him and bent to pet the Lab. His tail wagged wildly at the sight of her.

It was Willow's turn to feel a twisting pain inside. Uncle Hum was hers, hers and Twig's. How dare Sabrina call him Hum like that and say "Hi, Ho, Hum" instead of just "Hi."

"Willow coming here makes two girls who aren't teenagers or babies living on this road," Sabrina was babbling on. "Ten years I've waited for another girl my age! And here she is, at last."

Then Gram made the tension much worse by suggesting that Willow might like to walk Sabrina home.

"I'll look after Twig, don't worry," she said in a cheery voice that made Willow want to grab her brother and run out the door and keep on running until Gram was left far behind. "You girls should have some time to make friends, without trailing baby brothers along."

Willow was suddenly in such a panic that she could not speak. No words were there inside her head, only blazing anger and terror. Already Gram was separating her from Twig. They should never have come. Her fingers dug into Twig's skinny arm so hard that he yelped.

"Nell, stop rushing things," Uncle Hum said. "Willow

can walk Sabrina home if she feels like it, but I'm sure she'll want to take Twig along. He needs a little fresh air after that huge dose of television. Why don't you get his coat, Willow?"

Willow was trembling but, walking like a robot, she got Twig's coat down from its hook. Twig, realizing that he was going with the girls, brightened. Tiggy looked hopeful too.

"Not this time, Tig," Gram said gently. "I'm sorry, Willow. I don't know what I was thinking of. Don't take too long. I've got out a package of Kraft Dinner and some wieners."

Willow gave her a slightly wobbly but grateful smile. Gram knew that Twig was crazy about hot dogs and Kraft Dinner now that he had tried the real thing.

He skipped ahead of them once they were in the lane, splashing his new boots into every puddle he found, kicking pine cones, staring around at the astonishing emptiness of fields and hills.

"What's the matter with him?" Sabrina asked in a half-whisper. "I mean, he's not your average little kid, is he? You don't mind my asking, do you, Willow?"

Willow minded very much. This time, she longed to run back to the safety Gram made her feel. But she answered in a colourless voice.

"He's all right, just a bit slow. He was sick when he was a baby."

That was true enough. Willow shuddered, remembering how hard Twig had been to handle, how he had screamed and arched his body so it seemed his heels would touch the back of his head. Yet his deafness and strangeness were not Sabrina's business. She'd be bound to find out in time, but what was the rush? Willow needed to know her better first, find out how far to trust her.

"I'm adopted, you know," Sabrina volunteered out of the blue. She turned to stare into Willow's face as she went on telling family history. "It's a secret but I thought I'd tell you. They got me from a Russian orphanage."

For one stunned moment, Willow believed her. Then she saw the tell-tale signs. Angel had been a champion liar and Willow had watched her doing it for years. Sabrina was looking away. Her cheeks were flushed. She was talking in a voice a little too high and her words were spilling out far too fast.

When Willow said nothing, Sabrina swung around to glance at her face. Willow kept her expression blank.

"I am really," Sabrina insisted. "But don't mention it. My parents—my adoptive parents—don't want it known. Promise."

Willow looked at the other girl's hot cheeks and sparkling eyes. She had heard Angel tell wilder stories than this and had had to pretend her mother was telling the truth. She was not going to do it for anyone else. It made her feel ill. And it made everything too complicated.

"How old were you when you left Russia?" she asked casually, setting her trap.

"Just six," Sabrina said glibly. "I had my birthday on the ship."

"I don't get it. You said you'd lived on this road for ten years and you say you were six when you came. That makes you sixteen, not eleven," Willow said, keeping her voice low. She looked up at the trees as she spoke. She did not want to see Sabrina struggling to invent another lie.

Sabrina's breath came out in a hiss like air leaking from an inflatable mattress, but Willow ran before she could take a new breath in. She caught up with Twig. Tapping him on the shoulder, she pointed back at Stonecrop. He turned without a fuss, for once, and put his hand in hers. He was happy to be parting from the new girl who was taking his sister's attention. He shot Sabrina, who had begun to run away, a look of triumph.

He and Willow walked side by side toward their new home. Sabrina must have done an about-face once she was past them. Just in time, Willow caught the sound of her running feet coming right for them.

"Out of my way!" Sabrina shrieked. Willow jerked her brother aside as the strange girl careened past, running full-tilt, wild hair bouncing on the back of her neck. She was laughing loudly but it was put on, not real.

"What do you think you're doing?" Willow yelled after her. "You would have run him down if I hadn't grabbed him."

"Next time, let the baby watch out for himself," Sabrina's words, sharp and mean, were flung back at them like stones. She did not slow down for a second.

She was tearing across a field now, jumping over clumps of frozen earth, slipping and waving her arms wildly to keep herself from falling. She was crazy. The Jones kids watched her disappear behind a long line of dark evergreens. Then Willow went on walking home with her brother. But the sadness that filled her was no longer only for Twig and herself. Sabrina, too, needed that bridge over troubled water. She was not a Russian orphan but she was not an ordinary, everyday, well-loved eleven-year-old girl. What was wrong with her real family anyway?

"Wo! Wook!" Twig called, pointing out over the field.

Willow looked and saw three red cardinals and some other birds she did not recognize. The scarlet feathers blazed.

She shook off her confused thoughts about Sabrina and grinned at her small brother. His face shone. He had never seen such birds before. He probably did not remember those they had seen at Lou's cabin. He had never been in a place where he could stand and stare in perfect safety. They had been right to come. Now all they had to do was persuade Aunt Con that they should stay, and all their problems would be over. Except for Sabrina?

"I'll fix her," Willow muttered. "One way or another, I can take care of Miss Sabrina Marr."

14

Talk, Apple Peelings
and the School Bus

When she and Twig neared the front door of Stonecrop, Willow hesitated. She had run inside before, knowing she had to reach her brother, but she had not just calmly walked in without Gram going ahead or coming along behind. She, Willow, supposedly belonged here now but the front door, with its antique knocker, seemed to think she was a guest. She stood and looked at it, knowing Gram would tell her to stop being silly and yet anxious all the same.

"In," Twig said and opened the door.

Willow laughed and followed him.

"Good timing," Gram told them. "I was just coming to call you for supper. Con and Hum are eating downstairs tonight so it's just us."

Twig turned to go back to the TV. Willow put out a hand to catch him but he pulled free.

"Let him go," her grandmother said. "I've turned it off with the wall switch. He won't be able to make it work. I long ago found out that that saves a lot of arguing. Sit down, child, and set a good example."

Willow, feeling torn, sat down and braced herself. At the same time, she automatically speared the wiener already on her plate and took a giant bite. She was famished.

Then Twig blew in like a small tornado, bellowing with rage and frustration. He hurled himself at his sister. From the safety of her lap, he glared at his smiling grandmother.

"May ish fit," he yelled.

It made no sense but both Willow and his grandmother got the message. His sister bit her lip. Gram held out a bite of wiener.

"No, no, NO, NO!" Twig shrieked, trying to hit it out of her hand.

She backed out of range, shook her head at him and put the hot dog down on his plate. Then she got a big glass of juice and put it within reach.

"Look, Twig," Willow said loudly right into his ear. "Drink. I'll fix the TV after you drink."

Twig kicked a resounding tattoo on the table leg but he was very thirsty. Willow waited for the kicking to slow down and then lifted him bodily into his chair.

Twig, glowering, reached for the glass. He drank most of the juice and then deliberately stretched out his hand to pour the bit that was left onto Gram's plate. Gram saw it coming and snatched her dinner out of harm's way at the last second. Otherwise, she ignored him.

Willow had started to eat but she was having trouble

swallowing. She felt as though she could not bear it. If only he would . . .

Then, suddenly quiet and sweet, Twig picked up his fork and began to eat the Kraft Dinner as hungrily as Crocus had eaten his first full meal that morning. Willow, sighing with relief, took the first bite she really enjoyed.

The minute Twig started to slide down from his chair, Gram went swiftly ahead of him and, when he was not looking, she flipped the wall switch. He ran to the set to show her what was wrong and, to his astonished joy, the screen lit up.

"When you're in school, Willow, don't waste time stewing about what's going on here," Gram said quietly under cover of the sound of the TV. "The television is going to help me cope. So will Hum. Twig and he already like each other."

School! There it was again. Willow felt cold at the mere mention of it.

"What's the rush?" she muttered.

Yet she longed to go to school. It was what everybody did. Willow wanted to find out what it was like. Had Jo and Lou's teaching been enough?

"You need to discover where you fit before it breaks off for the summer," Gram said reasonably. "They're expecting you on Monday but you can wait if you don't feel ready."

Willow did not meet the steady gaze. She'd see. A little later, when the day was dimming into evening and the house felt chilly, Gram built a fire in the big fireplace in the back room and the family, people and animals both, were drawn to it. Twig, finally tired of sitting mesmerized by the TV screen, especially when the animated programs were no longer on, tagged after Willow. Uncle Hum went to a tall set of shelves and pulled out a couple of plastic bins filled with wooden blocks and Lego, little cars and various odds and ends of animals, trees, fence rails and even plastic people of several different kinds. Twig, enchanted, forgot about the TV and settled down to build himself a small kingdom.

Willow yearned to join him but resisted. He was happy without her, for once, and she liked watching the flames dance and nod. It reminded her of the fire demon in a book Lou had read aloud to her. She had loved that fire demon and, if she didn't stare too hard but stayed dreamy and almost asleep, she could catch glimpses of him looking out at her from Gram's fire. Nobody talked at first, even Aunt Con. Perhaps the effect of the fire was helped by Toby, curled up on her knee. Every so often, Gram got up to add a log. All the dogs watched her.

Crocus will love fires like this, Willow thought contentedly from deep inside the magic circle of peace.

"How did you and Sabrina hit it off?" Uncle Hum asked, breaking the spell.

"Fine, I guess," Willow said. She hesitated, looking down at her running shoes. Then she added quietly, "She . . . she said she was a Russian orphan."

She would not usually have told on another child that way but she needed to hear what he would say. She waited, relieved to have let the words be said in quiet firelight.

Aunt Con snorted.

"Orphan my foot," she said. "The Marrs have lived there ever since Mother sold the bulk of the farm. Even before that, they lived in this neighbourhood. The child even looks like Jem Marr. Remember her, Nell? She was in your class, wasn't she? Sabrina looks just like her."

"You're right," Gram said lazily. "I'd forgotten Jem's look of wildness. Too bad she isn't around more."

"It's not easy to drop in on the home place when you, your husband and all your children live in Yellowknife," Uncle Hum answered, his hand going down to scratch behind Sirius's satiny ear. "Even if she does look like her great-aunt, Sabrina must often feel like an orphan, Willow. She doesn't fit into the Marr family very well. They didn't adopt her, but her parents had a hard time when she was a baby. They were hoping for a boy, of course. They already had two girls. And they had a second set of twins, a boy and a girl. But the babies were premature, and the boy died. Sabrina weighed only three pounds and she didn't thrive even after they let Julia take her home from hospital. Her mother used to bring her over sometimes and sit and cry while our mother rocked the baby and told them both everything would be all right. I even rocked her myself, now and then, and she was hard to settle. I can still hear her cry. It pierced into your brain like . . . like a cross between a cat yowling and a fire engine."

"I remember that cry," Gram laughed.

Aunt Con sniffed. And Willow thought of Twig during his first few months. Uncle Hum had it right. That was exactly what Twig had sounded like sometimes. She felt a twinge of sympathy for Sabrina's mother. She knew how she had now and then longed to hurl Twig out the nearest window.

"You were a good baby and I'd have just put you down for a nap when Julia would arrive with Sabrina. I can remember praying her screams would not wake you up. They rarely did," Gram said. "Now I see that she was grieving over the death of the little boy but, at the time, I could not understand why she needed Mother so badly."

"Her grief took up so much room that she didn't have much attention left for Sabrina," said Uncle Hum. "It was Mother who named her. Did I ever tell you that, Nell? They'd picked out a whole list of boys' names but not one ready for a girl. Mother told me she chose it because the poor scrap needed a name that was old and strong and beautiful."

"But why . . . ?" Willow broke off her question, uncertain what she meant to say. She added lamely, "But all that was ten years ago. What's wrong now?"

Uncle Hum was the one who answered. "You're quite right. They should have recovered but, just before Sabrina turned five, Matthew was born. He was a beautiful, happy, healthy little boy and as fair as the twins. He's been the apple of their eye ever since. They all dote on him, except for Sabrina. First her twin's death and then her younger brother's birth turned her into an orphan."

"Rubbish. She's playing for sympathy and you're giving it to her. You and Nell should be telling her to snap out of it," Aunt Con's voice was loud and angry. "I'm sure they treat her just like the others, Humphrey. She's spoiled, if you ask me. Children are so manipulative."

Willow knew Aunt Con did not mean Sabrina Marr when she began talking about "spoiled children." But, for the first time, Willow agreed with her great-aunt. Sabrina was so lucky having two parents, twin sisters and a little brother who had nothing wrong with him. She should be thankful.

Twig looked up at Willow and, without warning, began to cry. He knocked over whatever he had built before she could see it. Then he grabbed two pieces of Lego and threw them at her.

"Hey!" Willow yelped as she ducked. She had had lots of practice. Before he could pick up more missiles to hurl, she leaped up and grabbed both his wrists.

"Bathtime," Gram said calmly. "You bring him and I'll go ahead and run the water."

Willow towed Twig up the stairs and was relieved to see that the warm water and the bathtub toys made him completely forget his rage. But, lying in bed herself, she went back to thinking about Sabrina. She sounded like a difficult friend.

I might be a difficult friend too, Willow said to herself.

The next day was Saturday. Willow did not see Sabrina. They went shopping for school clothes. Taking Twig made it far less fun than it should have been. But the wonderful new smell of clothes bought just for her was heady. Gram had trimmed her bangs properly and, in the store mirrors, she looked very unlike the ragamuffin she'd seen in the police station. When they got home, they made popcorn and watched *Babe*. Twig sat spellbound. Willow watched him and wished she knew what he was thinking.

On Sunday morning, Uncle Hum and Aunt Con went to church in Elora, the nearest town, but Gram and the children stayed home. Willow looked at her grandmother with troubled eyes.

"You go," she said. "We're okay on our own."

"I know," Gram said lightly. "But I need a Sunday off

every few weeks, and this is it. Next weekend, we can talk over what we'll do. This weekend, the church is not prepared for Twig nor Twig for the church."

Willow laughed and said no more. She was too worried to enjoy the day. Gram clearly expected her to get on that school bus the next morning and the thought of it made her feel sick. Abandoning Twig, who would not understand, was like a stony weight in her stomach.

But about two o'clock, when Twig was watching the video of *Babe* for the third time, she made up her mind to approach the non-Russian orphan.

"Gram," she blurted, "can I go over to Sabrina's for a few minutes?"

"Of course," Gram said. "It'll be easier on Monday if you've been together today. You'll ride the same school bus, you know."

Willow went out the front door and turned to cut across the snowy side yard without answering. Words stuck in her throat. One minute Gram said she could wait until she was ready and the next she was pushing her out the door. Onto a school bus! She had never ridden in one. Would they be expecting her? Where would she sit?

She reached the Marrs' house before she could sort out her tumbling thoughts. It looked as though nobody was home. She stared at the silent house and almost turned tail and ran.

"Hey, Willow!"

The voice came from behind her. Willow spun around and saw Sabrina standing in the open doorway of the big barn. They stood very still for a few seconds, eyeing each other. Then, not knowing what else to do, Willow raised one hand and gave a sketchy wave.

Instantly Sabrina began to run toward her in big jumping steps.

Like a kangaroo, Willow thought, remembering one she and Twig had seen on Gram's TV.

Right in front of her, near enough to touch, Sabrina stopped bounding.

"What do you want?" she asked, her voice rough, her eyes guarded but hopeful.

"I never rode in a school bus before," Willow said, thinking it was as good a place to start as any other. "How do you know where to sit?"

"You can sit by me," Sabrina said, turning a little and staring over at Stonecrop. "Where's your brother?"

"Watching *Babe*. Who do you sit with now?"

"Nobody. I like sitting by myself."

Willow was about to say, "Fine. I won't bother you then," when she remembered that Sabrina was the only girl her age along this stretch of road.

"Thanks," she said.

"Come on in. My mum wants to meet you. We might as well get it over with," said Sabrina, pushing past Willow and shoving the back door open with a wham from her mittened hand.

A small, thin woman sat at the kitchen table peeling apples. When she looked up, Willow saw her eyes were not the grey-green of the ocean but the plain blue of the sky. Washed out a bit, she noted. Her hair was smooth and fair, not washed out at all. And her smile was friendly.

"This is Willow," Sabrina said, and then nodded her head towards her mother. "She's my mum."

As she named the relationship, Sabrina's ocean-coloured eyes met Willow's, daring her to mention Russia. Willow looked back squarely for a long moment, not smiling. Then she turned and spoke politely to Mrs. Marr. She even put out her hand before she realized that the woman's hands were occupied. She put her hand hastily behind her and felt her cheeks grow hot.

"Well, I've been waiting for a chance to meet you, Willa," Mrs. Marr said warmly. "Your grandmother is so happy to have you here. She called before you arrived to order extra eggs and to see if we had any of Matthew's outgrown clothes for your little brother. It will be so nice for Matthew to have a playmate right next door. When she came for the things, she was all excited about meeting your plane in the morning. I don't think she got much sleep. The lights were still on over there when I looked out my bedroom window at two."

"Her name is Willow," Sabrina said, breaking in on the nervous flood of words and stressing the second syllable. She began to say something about Twig's not being a bit like Matthew. She caught the words back though and stared at the apple her mother had just finished peeling.

Mrs. Marr had done it all in one long spiral of peel, translucent and amazing. Reaching to take it from the table, Sabrina astounded Willow by twirling it around her head three times and letting it drop over her left shoulder. Then she and her mother stared down at it.

"It's a G," Sabrina announced, looking up and meeting the

other girl's surprised stare with a grin. "I'm going to marry a man whose name begins with G."

"What?" Willow said.

Sabrina reached for the next long peel curling from her mother's paring knife. She held it out.

"Try it," she said. "Twirl it three times and then drop it over your shoulder."

Willow, a little nervous, followed instructions. The peeling broke as it hit the floor. She giggled.

"I'm going to marry two of them," she said, staring at the apple skin curls. "And they're both zeros."

Matthew ran in, at that moment, his cheeks pink, his blue eyes bright with excitement.

"The new calf's a heifer," he announced.

"Oh, yeah. I forgot," Sabrina mumbled. "Dad said to tell you. Come on, Willow. Let's go to my room."

Willow took one last glance at the apple peelings on the floor before she picked them up and put them on the table edge. Then she followed Sabrina without even stopping to take off her coat.

From the moment Matthew had come through the door, his mother had ceased to notice either of the girls so it didn't matter. When she went home half an hour later, neither of them had mentioned Sabrina's lie but Willow knew they were going to be friends.

The next morning, Gram walked out to the end of the lane with Willow while Uncle Hum kept Twig busy playing with his computer keyboard. It was warmer than it had been the day before. Willow looked back and waved to the dogs clustered on the wide window sills.

"They'll be watching for you at four o'clock," Gram said. "They won't let the bus pass without announcing it."

Willow could not think of anything to say. She was afraid she might throw up. She struggled not to imagine Twig searching the house for her but she could not keep the scene from playing over and over inside her mind.

"I'm going to take him to see the kittens across the road," Gram said as though she could see into Willow's private thoughts. "And we'll go to Sears and get him a garage and some Dinky trucks. And there's lots of TV. I'll bring him with me to meet the bus. Don't worry, big sister. Twig Jones will be my one concern all day long."

Willow felt the weight of worry inside her lift, the darkness lighten. Twig would be all right until she came back. She looked up the lane and along the road. Matthew Marr, neatly and warmly clad in a jacket, splash pants, boots, mittens and a knitted hat, was trotting toward the end of the Marrs' drive with his mother coming behind him carrying his backpack.

A large, dirty yellow bus came churning through the mud toward them. Where was Sabrina? Suddenly, coat open, scarf flapping, boots unzipped, no gloves or hat, backpack thumping against her shoulders, she came leaping after the others. She had told Willow the day before that her sisters went early to rehearse for some concert.

"Hey, Willow Jones, I'll beat you to the bus," Sabrina yelled, coming on even faster and shooting past her mother and small brother.

Willow had no intention of plunging onto the bus for the first time looking as wild as her new friend. Matthew, in a sudden panic, shrieked, "Wait! Sabrina, wait for me!"

Sabrina was almost at the bus. She didn't so much as glance back.

"We're waiting," Willow called to the small boy. "Don't worry. We won't leave without you."

"He knows," Sabrina said disgustedly. "What a wimpy baby!"

But she stopped and boosted the little boy up the steps. Matthew turned and reached out to his mother, who handed over his lunchbox.

"Bye-bye, sweetheart," she said. "Be a good boy and learn lots."

Matthew nodded and clumped to one of the front seats. Willow shot her grandmother a farewell look but said nothing. Gram gave a quick wave and turned away without making embarrassing speeches.

"Here's Sappy," one of the boys murmured in a voice pitched too low for the driver to hear. "Who's your friend, Sap? Pocahontas?"

"Ignore the vermin," Sabrina told Willow, sliding over to make room for her. "Patrick can't help it. He was asleep when the brains were given out."

Willow shot a fast look at Patrick. He was a dark boy, his skin nearly the same brown as her own, and he wore round glasses. They looked just like a pair of zeros.

The Grade Five teacher, Miss de Vries, was really nice. Strict but fair. She was interested in what kids told her. She looked at Willow exactly the way she looked at all the white kids in the class. She didn't seem to see that there was a difference, let alone be bothered by it. And she said "Willow" right off the bat.

"What a lovely name," she said, looking down at her book. "Willow Wind. I've had a Brooke, two Summers, a Stardust and a Stormy. But I think Willow is the best. I like names with meaning."

Willow thought about Uncle Star, Angel, and Calypso-Twig, but kept her mouth firmly closed. Miss de Vries must have guessed that it was a sensitive subject because she spoke in a low voice only Willow could hear. Then she asked about Willow's previous schooling.

Willow told her as much as she could. Miss de Vries had her read aloud to her and work out some math problems. If it had not been for Jo and Lou's teaching and their library, she knew she would have been far behind. But she had worked hard on correspondence courses when she could and read every time she had a moment to herself. Math was her weak point. Yet she knew the basic arithmetic facts and could solve problems.

"It sounds as though you're going to be my favourite kind of student," the teacher smiled. "You'll go right on learning whatever happens. You have a hungry mind."

"I guess so," Willow muttered and went back to sit next to Sabrina.

She glanced sidewise at the class, all various shades of white. She had never seen a roomful of kids all one colour before. Too bad Patrick wasn't in here.

"Good morning, Patrick," Miss de Vries said, making Willow jump. "How can you manage to come on the bus and still be late?"

"Just talent," the boy said, grinning.

"Try to cultivate some of your other gifts in future," said

Miss de Vries, her tone teasing, her eyes serious.

"I'll give it a whirl," Patrick said. He added, "I had to stop by the library. I needed a book on black holes."

He waved a book at the teacher and sat down. He was two seats away from Willow and Sabrina. Having him there, his glasses slipping down his nose, his hair soon standing up in tufts because he constantly tousled it with the hand that did not hold a pen, made Willow feel more at home.

She barely heard the lessons after lunch in her eagerness to be gone. As the bus turned up the 6th Line, she craned her neck. Yes, Gram was there and so was Twig, pulling on her hand, trying to run to the bus and being held in check against his will.

And right behind them stalked Crocus, home from the vet and obviously feeling himself to be the cat of the house.

15
"I'm Eleven."

The first week of school passed. Willow discovered that she was ahead of the rest in reading and language but behind in math. She had never played the games they did and she did not understand their slang. But Sabrina was quick to stand up for her whenever she seemed to need it and she survived. It even grew easier as the weekend neared.

Nobody mentioned Willow's birthday. Willow herself wondered if she should remind Gram but she hesitated. Gram had given her so much, new clothes, books she loved, the willow quilt. She needed nothing else and, if she told Gram she was turning eleven on Saturday, her grandmother might think she was expecting presents.

"Don't hint," Angel had commanded her when she had tried to get Julius to give her money for the gum machine. "It's not fair. If you want something, come right out with it so the person knows what you're after. And remember what my mother said."

Willow knew what she meant. She'd heard it often.

If wishes were horses, than beggars would ride.
If wishes were fishes, we'd have some fried.

I've never had birthday presents, she thought, nor a cake with candles. I shouldn't miss them. She'd never been to a birthday party either. Or had she? Somewhere, in the depths of her dim memories, four candles flickered and then—poof!—went out.

You have so, Red Mouse said. I remember. You blew all the candles out but one and Angel said that meant you were going to get one special wish.

Willow wanted to argue but she, too, saw that lone candle burning when the others went out. They weren't on a proper birthday cake though. Was it a pie? She thought maybe. A frozen blueberry one. She had been so careful what she wished for, wanting to get it for sure.

What did I wish for? she asked Red Mouse.

You didn't tell me, Red Mouse said. Wishes don't come true if you blab them to mice.

Willow chuckled. Red Mouse was good at coaxing her out of what Gram called "a fit of the dismals."

But on Friday night she went to bed wondering if her birthday would be noticed by anybody. She had told Sabrina the day they met. Maybe Sabrina would recall the date. Willow doubted it somehow. Sabrina wasn't the kind of girl who remembered things like dates, especially when they weren't her own.

When she woke up, Willow saw that the sky was pink and luminous like a birthday sky ought to be. A bird was singing in the apple tree beneath her window. She got out of bed and slipped across the room to peer out, looking for whoever was singing to her.

A robin sat in the tree, head thrown back, carolling for all he was worth. Willow grinned. His song was her first present. She'd watch for others.

Twig bounced out of his bottom bunk and beamed at her. His curls were tangled and his eyes still looked drowsy but his face lit up with joy at a new day about to begin.

"It's my birthday," she told him, knowing he would not understand. "I'm eleven."

"Go, go, Wo," he urged, starting out the door. "Ju'."

Willow followed him, feeling shy and as though she had just arrived from Vancouver and didn't know anyone at Stonecrop. She got three steps down the main staircase when Gram started to sing, "Happy birthday to you."

By the time she got to the end, Uncle Hum's voice was sounding out from the basement stairs. Even Aunt Con, clearly surprised but not wanting to be left out, was joining in.

Willow stood still and felt her face grow hot with pleasure and embarrassment.

"Come on down, birthday girl," Gram called, smiling at her from the foot of the stairs.

"How did you know?" Willow croaked.

"I was there. I only missed seeing you get born by about fifteen minutes. How could I forget? You were the newest person I'd ever met."

She told the whole story of Willow's birth while she

167

poured in waffle batter. Willow sat and listened, enthralled. Twig watched the waffle iron impatiently.

At her place at the table a pile of wrapped gifts waited. Earrings like tiny unicorns. Angel had had Willow's ears pierced when she was six. A new book. A sweat shirt which Uncle Hum had had printed especially. On the front it said READING IS THE BEST BAD HABIT. There was a video and two CDs. There was a wooden chess board from Gram, who was teaching Willow to play chess, and a wooden cribbage board from Uncle Hum, who had promised to teach her to play.

And there was a jewel case from Aunt Con. It had been hastily wrapped and Willow had seen it on Aunt Con's dresser with necklaces spilling out of it. So what! As Angel also said, "It's not the thought, it's the deed that counts." In this, Willow agreed with her mother.

The last present was a copy of Elspet Gordon's account of her life as a pioneer girl coming to Nichol Township in 1841. Willow turned the pages, gazing spellbound at the neat writing, so unlike anything she could do. They had copied the original and had it bound so that she could keep it.

"Thank you," she breathed.

"I think you and Elspet Mary have a lot in common," Gram said.

They were about to have lunch when Uncle Hum told Willow he had another gift for her. It was by far the largest present she had ever received. She unwrapped it not knowing what to expect. It was a beanbag chair for the room she and Twig shared. The moment she got the last of the paper pulled free, Toby and Panda were up and in, snuggling down.

"The darlings," Aunt Con cooed.

And, for once, Willow agreed with her.

Sabrina came for supper.

"Next year you can have a proper party," Gram said.

Willow's heart sang. It sounded so sure. Next year she would be here and she would know enough kids to have a party. But she was glad her grandmother had not gone and invited anyone else this time.

There was a cake, three-layer marble with seven-minute icing. Sabrina had brought Willow three different colours of nail polish and they painted their toenails Ebony and their fingernails Midnight Blue. Twig chose Tropical Pink for his.

The whole day was amazing and perfect until Willow was about to go up to bed. Gram met her at the top of the stairs and handed her a last box. She was smiling in a way that told her granddaughter that this present, if that was what it was, was one Gram thought she would love.

"I've saved this until we were alone. It's my best surprise for you," her grandmother said.

Willow looked down at the box and felt uneasy. She had no idea why. She couldn't guess what was inside. But it was an old box wrapped in brown paper and tied with string. WILLOW was written on the paper but the word had not been written yesterday or even a month ago. The ink had had time to fade and the parcel smelled old.

"Here. I'll cut the string for you," Gram said. "Those knots would take forever to untie."

She snipped through the string with nail scissors and gathered the bits into her hand. Then the phone rang. Aunt Con got it. She was always the first to get to the phone and always disgruntled because it was so seldom someone calling her. The note of disgust was clear as she called, "Nell, it's for you."

Gram swore.

"Take it into your room," she said. "There's enough light from Twig's night light for you to see. I'll come as soon as I can get away. The trouble is I'm expecting a call from a friend who has some family problem she wants to tell me about. I wish I could see your face . . . but you go ahead."

Willow went into the room she and Twig still shared and sat down in the beanbag chair. Slowly, very slowly, she removed three layers of paper. Then she took a deep breath and lifted the lid.

Wrapped in tissue paper was a doll. It was a baby doll with wide blue eyes and pink cheeks and a sweet smile. Her arms were bent up as though she was reaching out to Willow. And Willow remembered her perfectly.

"Lucinda," she whispered. "She kept Lucinda."

Then rage boiled up in her and, without glancing at Twig, fast asleep in the bottom bunk, she hurled the doll across the room.

"I'm eleven," she said through shut teeth. "I'm eleven and I haven't played with dolls since . . . since . . . "

Tears began running down her cheeks. She was herself at four, so lonely, missing her Gram terribly. They were in the bus station in Guelph when she realized Lucinda had been left behind.

"I have to go back," she had cried, overjoyed at the knowledge. "I forgot Lucinda."

Angel had looked down at her coldly.

"Who's Lucinda?" she had asked.

"My doll," Willow had explained, beginning to tug on her mother's arm. "I need her. I have to go back for her."

"I'll get you another doll," Angel had said. "Forget Lucinda. We aren't going back there—now or ever. Your grandmother told me never to darken her door again."

Willow had become hysterical then and ended up being slapped across the cheek and told to shut up or she'd be sorry.

Gram had let Angel take her and keep her away and, all the time, she had kept Lucinda safe. What made Lucinda so precious? She should have kept Willow, not a dumb doll.

Sobs wracked Willow. She had started and she thought she would never be able to stop. She had not been given another doll, not a proper one she could love. Julius had found some Barbies at a garage sale but Willow had never played with them. There was no love in their grown-up, glamorous faces.

And then, of course, she had had Twig.

The sobs quieted as she thought of trying to cuddle Twig when he was Lucinda's size. Lucinda had been much easier to handle but Lucinda had never been real.

She was real when you were four, Red Mouse said.

Willow got out of the beanbag chair and put on her pajamas. Lucinda still lay, face down, dress tumbled up over her head, in front of the chest of drawers.

Willow knew it was time to brush her teeth. She decided her teeth needed a vacation. She climbed up into the upper bunk and lay there, her face set, her eyes burning.

But she could still see Lucinda from where she lay. It wasn't Lucinda's fault, any of it.

Finally, unable to stop herself, Willow slid down from her

bunk and picked up the doll. She sat her in the beanbag chair and stood looking down at her. Then she picked her up and gave her a tight hug.

"I wanted you so much," she whispered. "But it's too late. I'm eleven and I don't play with dolls."

Then she set Lucinda back in the beanbag chair and got back into bed. By the time Gram tiptoed in at last, she was asleep. Gram, looking up at her, saw the telltale marks of tears on her face. She saw Lucinda in the chair and hesitated.

At last, she picked up the box and almost replaced the doll in it. Then, taking the box, she left the room without moving the doll from the chair.

When Twig wakened, he raced across to the chair and picked up the doll. He rocked her back and forth in his arms.

"Beebee," he called up to Willow. "Beebee."

Willow rubbed her hands over her face to wake herself up and smiled down at him.

"She's for you," she told him.

He brought the doll down to breakfast. He showed her to Gram.

"Mine," he said. "Beebee mine."

Willow did not meet Gram's eyes.

"Twig's four," she said, her voice cool. "I'm eleven now."

Gram sighed.

"You're right," she said. "I'd have sent her to you, Willow, but I had no idea where you were for months. And, when I did know, I'd put her away. But I did keep her safe."

Dolls can't be hurt, Willow thought, bitterness choking her again. I was the one you should have kept safe.

She was sure she had not said the words aloud. Maybe Gram could read thoughts.

"You're right," she said. "You were the one I should have fought to keep. I let you go . . . and I've regretted it ever since. But you weren't my child."

There was a stretched, miserable silence, broken only by Twig's murmuring to Lucinda. Then Willow pushed the bitterness away.

"You should have kept me safe," she said, "but you took me back the minute I phoned you. And you took Twig too."

Their eyes met. The look they exchanged was not quite a smile but almost. Willow thought of hugging Gram but her hurt over the doll was too raw and recent.

"Here," Gram said, handing her a glass of orange juice. "Drink that fast and get on with your breakfast or you'll be late for the bus."

"It's Sunday," Willow said. "No school bus today."

"Right. Only the Gram Van to take us all to church."

"Church . . . " Willow said uncertainly.

"Church," her grandmother said firmly. "Elora United Church. You went there with me when you were small. You were in the Nursery. They know we're coming."

Willow contented herself with a nod. Words like "God" and "Jesus" had been swear words in the company she had kept in Vancouver. But she remembered knowing that they really meant something totally different.

As she got up to put her empty orange juice glass in the sink, she remembered her birthday. She was well into her new book already and she loved it. It had been from Gram. And Gram had made the cake and given her the new school outfit.

Angel, on the other hand, had rarely remembered her daughter's birthday. When she had, it had been to complain that Willow was growing old too fast.

On her way back to her chair, Willow reached out and gave her grandmother a flying hug from behind, one Gram was in no position to return. By the time Gram had poured two glasses of milk, Willow was back on her chair, eating her cereal as though she were in a race.

"Eleven years old," Gram said softly. "I'll remember."

Willow stood in the church singing,

> There is a balm in Gilead
> That makes the wounded whole.
> There is a balm in Gilead
> That heals the sin sick soul.

They should have called Stonecrop "Gilead," she thought. Then Twig escaped from the Nursery and began racing up and down the aisles. That ended any reverie. But, even when he was being his worst self, the people smiled at the two children. Uncle Hum produced jujubes from his pocket and Gram got paper and crayons out of her purse and peace descended once more.

16
Out Cold

Willow and Twig and Crocus had lived at Stone-crop for nearly a month when Aunt Con fell down the stairs.

Even Twig, intent on "The Polka Dot Door," heard her land. The house shook. The crash sounded deafening, and more frightening still was the utter silence that followed it. Willow was sitting on the couch reading a book and petting Crocus at the same time. Crocus sprang to the floor, fur standing up in alarm, and Willow dropped her book and sat frozen for an instant. Then she and Twig leaped up and ran to see what had happened.

Aunt Con was lying all in a heap at the foot of the long staircase. Her head was bleeding and one of her legs was twisted under her. She was not moaning, not twitching, but, to Willow's relief, she did seem to be breathing. Her chest moved ever so slightly. Her eyes were closed.

"Boom," Twig said.

His sister ignored him. She dropped to her knees beside the still figure.

"Aunt Con, are you all right?" she cried, bending over her and searching for some sign of the grouchy aunt she was used to.

Aunt Con did not stir. Twig reached out and touched her cheek with one finger.

"Ow, ow," he moaned softly, his eyes huge, his mouth quivering.

Willow jumped up and ran for the towel hanging in the bathroom. She had seen a first-aid movie once. She remembered that you should stop the bleeding, cover the patient and not move her and get help. With shaking hands, she folded the towel and pressed it as firmly as she dared against the cut on Aunt Con's forehead. It was swelling up into a lump now. As Willow pressed, the bleeding was staunched and her great-aunt moaned.

"Aunt Con!" Willow shouted, her relief enormous. "Aunt Con, you're alive."

"Of course, I'm alive," the injured woman said thickly and opened her eyes. She stared blurrily at the girl's face bending close to hers. "Who are you? Where am I?"

"You're here," Willow said, pushing Twig's hand back from Aunt Con's cheek. "I mean, we're at home. You fell down the stairs. Just lie still and I'll get help."

"Nell . . . Get Nell," the thick voice said.

Willow didn't wait to remind Aunt Con that Gram and Uncle Hum had driven in to town to do a bunch of errands. She ran and dialled the number Gram had written up for

Emergency. When a cool voice answered, she did her best to relate what had happened. The voice seemed to ask a hundred questions. Willow was thankful that she had heard Gram giving directions to people on how to reach Stonecrop. She rattled off what she remembered, hoping all the time that Twig wasn't pestering their injured aunt and that Aunt Con herself was remaining still.

"Somebody will be there within twenty minutes," the voice said crisply and the line went dead.

Willow took a deep breath and tried to slow her hammering heart. Then she dashed back, struggling to remember what else the first-aid video had said. What she saw made her stare.

Aunt Con was actually smiling at Twig, who was offering her a drink from one of the juice glasses. He had spilled a lot of water over himself and some onto Aunt Con but he was now holding it to her lips and, to Willow's astonishment, she tried to drink. They were all surprised when her teeth chattered against the rim. Willow bit back a hysterical burst of laughter and then relaxed as she saw Aunt Con laugh herself. The girl knelt and steadied the tumbler while her great-aunt drained it.

"Good. The bleeding has stopped," Willow muttered, as she lifted the towel enough to peer at the wound underneath.

Then Twig was back with a seedless green grape.

"Ope, ope," he ordered, pressing it against Aunt Con's lips.

When she opened her lips to speak, he popped the grape into her mouth, jumped up and ran away back to the kitchen.

"Good," Aunt Con said and chewed. Before Willow could

think what to do next, her little brother was back with a single potato chip.

"Ope," he commanded.

Aunt Con hastily swallowed what was left of the grape and opened her mouth obediently. In went the potato chip.

Twig beamed. Willow pulled herself together, recalled you were supposed to keep the patient warm and ran for a wool blanket.

"He's dear," Aunt Con said shakily as Willow spread the blanket over her and tucked in the sides. Without meaning to, she joggled the leg which was still bent up in an unnatural angle. Aunt Con gasped and let out a small whimper.

"I'm sorry," Willow said. "Did I hurt you?"

"No, but don't bump into me. Nell? Where's Nell?"

"She's gone to town. She should be home soon. But I called for an ambulance," Willow told her.

"You should have waited. Nell's a nurse," Aunt Con murmured and let her eyes close.

Twig lay down on the carpet next to her, covered himself up with a shawl from the living room and closed his eyes too. Toby and Panda, who had been watching from a few feet away, moved in and curled up between the two of them, making themselves cosy. Tiggy trotted over and pressed against Willow as though she knew the girl felt suddenly small and alone. Willow put her cheek down against Tiggy's solid body and took comfort from her. Tiggy gently licked her cheek. They all waited in silence.

Then Aunt Con's eyes opened. Willow sat up fast.

"Mother . . ." the woman said.

"It's me, Willow. You fell down the stairs," Willow said,

talking quickly because she was frightened. "What made you fall, Aunt Con? You were unconscious."

"Don't let Nell send me away," Aunt Con whispered.

Her eyes closed again. Willow gulped. She wished somebody would come.

Then Aunt Con's eyes popped wide open once more and she stared at the children as though she had never seen them before.

"I want to sit up now," she announced in a much stronger voice. "What's going on here? My head hurts. Help me up, girl."

"No," Willow told her, sounding as much like Gram as she could. "Just lie still and breathe deeply until someone comes."

Aunt Con did not argue, although she did give a giant, exasperated sigh before she gave in. Twig stayed where he was but his eyes were open now. Every time Aunt Con groaned, Twig groaned with her. After the third groan, she laughed. But it was a very weary laugh.

Then Willow heard the ambulance turning down the lane, its siren shattering the peace of the afternoon.

Twig hovered, eyes wide, while Aunt Con was strapped onto a stretcher and carried out to the ambulance. Willow closed the door behind them and sank down on the bottom step. Twig turned and gazed at her. Then, his eyes full of anxiety, he ran and brought her a glass of water too.

"Wo, ope," he said proudly.

Willow smiled and took the cup. She found she was as thirsty as her great-aunt had been. She pleased him by draining the cup and holding it out for more.

Fifteen minutes later, Gram's van pulled up in front of the door. Both children rushed to meet the two grown-ups. Willow discovered, to her surprise, that now the waiting was over and everything was going to be taken care of, tears began to run down her face. She ignored them.

Gram, about to open the rear door of the van and get out the groceries, stared at her granddaughter.

"What on earth . . . ?" she began.

"Aunt Con's in the hospital," Willow sobbed. "She fell down the stairs. I had to call the ambulance."

Twig was hopping up and down, doing his best to tell about the water and food he had given her.

"Poor Willow," Gram said, hugging her close. "It sounds as though you've done a great job. Let's go in and then you can tell me everything from the beginning."

Willow told all she could remember.

"I thought she might be dead," she managed, shivering at the memory.

"Not tough old Connie," Uncle Hum said. "It's a long way down those stairs, mind you, but she'll be fine. Not only that but she'll positively love being an invalid."

"Maybe they'll send her to a nursing home," Gram said.

"She doesn't want to be sent away," Willow said. "I'll look after her dogs. I promised. You should have seen Twig."

She told them about Twig's offerings.

"She called him 'dear,'" she finished.

"Good work, Twig," Gram said. "I presume they took her to Fergus?"

Willow nodded.

"I'd better go and see what's happening," Gram said.

"Hum, you're in charge. Do your best not to break your leg while I'm away. If you do, you are definitely going to a nursing home."

She was gone a long time. Uncle Hum scrambled eggs and made lots of toast for supper. Then he took Twig up for his bath. Willow, anxiously watching the front door, left him to it. Nothing was said about his having any problem until about fifteen minutes had passed. Then Twig began to shriek.

Willow ran up to see what was wrong. Uncle Hum was drying Twig, who appeared to be unhurt but very excited. Willow groaned inwardly. It was hard getting him to sleep when he got wound up.

"He feels awfully slippery," Uncle Hum said.

Willow glanced into the tub. Uncle Hum had put in bubble bath but that was not all that was in the water.

"What are those things?" she asked, pointing, totally forgetting he could not see much.

"Those things? What do you mean?" Uncle Hum asked, standing up and carrying Twig to their room.

Gram arrived home at that moment and whatever was in the tub was forgotten. Aunt Con had broken a bone in her ankle and was covered with bruises. Her head wound was not serious. That night, her leg was put into a cast and she was drugged into a deep sleep.

"We'll go and visit in the morning," Gram promised.

Nobody else bothered with a bath that night. In the morning, when Twig got up, every curl on his head was rigid. When he shook his head, his hair actually rattled.

"What on earth . . . ?" Gram said.

"There was something in the bath water," Willow remembered. "It was like a bunch of giant jellyfish. I forgot when you came home. Did you run out the water?"

"Not I," her grandmother said, going to investigate. Willow went along, curious to learn what those things were.

They were still there. Gram stared at them.

"I know this is ridiculous but they look like Metamusil," she mused.

Uncle Hum, standing in the doorway, swore he had put in nothing but bubble bath.

"Where is your . . . ?" Willow started to ask.

Gram looked across at the table next to the sink. A bottle sat there. It had no lid. The label read Metamusil. But the bottle was empty.

"It was almost full. Hum, how could you have mixed it up with bubble bath?" Gram cried.

"He didn't," Willow said. "I saw the bubbles myself. I think . . . maybe . . . Twig was trying to help?"

She waited, breath held, for the explosion. Gram did make a strange, strangling noise, but she was laughing.

"That boy! How will I ever get it out of his hair?" she said, wiping her eyes.

"With difficulty," said Twig's great-uncle.

It made a great story to tell Aunt Con when they got to the hospital. They were late because of it. Twig's hair had been shampooed four times and there were still a few stubborn spikes. Cleaning the bathtub was another ordeal. The muck was even inside the rubber ducks.

If Gram doesn't send us away after this, Willow told herself, we're here for good.

Aunt Con was up, seated in a reclining chair with her legs propped up.

"You look as though you've been in a war," Willow said, impressed by her aunt's bandaged head and visible bruises.

"I feel that way too. But the doctor says I can come home," Aunt Con said, doing her best to sound confident.

Willow looked at her grandmother. Was she going to say Aunt Con had to go to a nursing home? If she did, how could Willow make her understand that Aunt Con was afraid?

"Can you walk?" Gram asked bluntly.

"On crutches," Aunt Con said. "But I'm sure I can manage just fine, Nell. I'll be no trouble."

Gram snorted.

"When will you be signed out?" she asked.

The enormous relief on Aunt Con's face made Willow look away. Her eyes met her grandmother's.

"Yes, yes, Willow. I got your message," she said. "Although I don't for one moment believe it'll be easy. I'll go ask at the desk when we can take her."

She strode out of the room. Twig had discovered how to raise and lower the foot and head of the bed and was busily doing so. Up, down, up, down. It was perfect.

Aunt Con and Willow were silent, listening to Gram's swift footsteps and the whir of the motor that adjusted the bed. Then, all at once, the injured woman turned and reached out, clutching Willow's hand.

"You'll help me, won't you?" she begged, squeezing the fingers she held. "I won't be able to go up and down stairs. I'll need . . . oh, lots of help. But I don't want Nell to have to bother. If it weren't for your help yesterday and that dear

183

little brother of yours, wild though he is, I don't know what would have happened. Promise you'll help."

"I promise," said Willow Wind Jones.

She grinned suddenly. It looked as though she and Twig would be staying for a few weeks longer, at least. As long as she could keep the Metamusil out of his reach and prevent his damaging one of the darling boys. That shouldn't be too hard.

17
Night, nigh'

Aunt Con made a terrible invalid. Willow was kept running for things her great aunt said she needed immediately. Sometimes, Willow suspected, Aunt Con didn't need the things as much as she needed company.

"Could you bring me my nail scissors?" she would ask. "They're in the drawer of my bedside table. Be sure and hook the door shut so your brother won't get in there."

Luckily, Twig could not yet manage to undo the safety hooks Gram had put on all the bedroom doors and the upstairs bathroom. He got into plenty of trouble as it was. Aunt Con soon almost forgot how dear he was and remembered he was a nuisance she wanted to evict from the house.

Willow's biggest concern, however, was for the two papillons. They were such delicate little dogs but they were also lively and inquisitive and Twig adored chasing them from room to room. He seemed incapable of realizing that what was a glorious game to him was terrifying to them. At least, Aunt Con believed they were terrified. A couple of times, Willow had noticed that when Twig was caught and made to stop, the tiny dogs came looking for him, their feathery tails quivering, their eyes bright. He never caught them. They could run like the wind and they could scamper under furniture and emerge on the other side while he was down on his stomach looking for them.

They also were great snugglers and when Aunt Con grew impatient with them, they would run to the couch where Twig sprawled, mesmerized by television, and curl up next to him. He would stroke them absent-mindedly and his jumpiness would calm down until they were all drowsing together.

Seeing them that way, Willow came up with something new to stew about. What if Twig won the darling boys' hearts away from their mistress, who, at the moment, never took them for walks or played ball with them?

Don't be dumb, she told herself sternly. He won't, they won't and she won't.

But once she had seen the danger, she kept watch for a blow-up whenever she was in the house. She almost failed to notice the days growing warmer, the crocuses being replaced by tulips, the lawns turning vivid green with the coming of new grass. Almost. Right outside her window was a big apple tree and, when it blossomed, she forgot Twig and Aunt Con and everything that had come before in her life for a few rapt minutes. She threw up the window and breathed in the fragrance. She felt like Anne Shirley looking out at the cherry tree she named the Snow Queen.

Yet that was the very afternoon when she came home to

find nobody there to meet her. And, as she and Sabrina halted at the end of the lane to bask in the beauty of the spring afternoon, she heard Twig screaming inside the house, screaming as though someone was trying to throttle him.

Willow ran.

She did not hear Sabrina running after her or notice when her thudding footsteps slowed and then stopped. Sabrina Marr, for once in her life, knew she should not intrude on whatever was about to happen in her new friend's home.

When Willow threw open the inside door and catapulted into the hall, she saw nobody. Twig's shrieks were mounting, however, and she had no trouble finding him. He was lying flat on his back on the living-room floor, his face dark with fury and awash with tears and he was kicking at Gram, who was bending over him. He was obviously doing his best to hit her whenever she seemed to be coming within range of his wildly flailing arms.

Gram's lips were moving but it was impossible to make out a word she was saying. She, too, was red in the face and she, too, looked as though she wanted to hit somebody.

Willow knew exactly how she was feeling. She grabbed her grandmother's arm and pulled. Gram's head jerked up and she glared at the interruption until she saw it was Willow. She began trying to explain. Willow pulled harder, dragged her back into the hall from which she herself had just come and slammed the door loudly so that Twig would be sure to notice.

"Willow, I swear to you that I don't know what is wrong," Gram began, her voice shaking with a mixture of wrath and embarrassment at being found in such a rage.

"Don't worry. You never know when it's going to happen. And he can't stop himself, not till it has . . . blown over. Sit down, Gram. He's already beginning to cry."

"Beginning to cry . . . ." Gram said, outraged. "He's been crying ever since we got home from the audiologist."

Willow went very still. So Gram had taken him for a hearing test, had she? Why hadn't she said they were going? But she made herself finish what she had been about to say.

"That was screaming. He's beginning to stop screaming and start crying. There's a big difference. Once he begins to cry instead of scream, I can get him to stop, I think. We just have to wait another minute or two. What happened at the ear doctor's?"

Gram's face lit up and then, as quickly, clouded again.

"She tested his hearing, which wasn't easy. We had to watch for him to turn his head when he heard a beep. He has severe hearing loss in the one ear, just as you thought. The other ear also has significant loss but not as bad. Then we went over to the hearing aid place and the woman there made impressions of his ears. It didn't take long and he ate a lollipop while she did it. But he was clearly edgy. When we came out to the car and he finished the sucker, he suddenly began to screech at the top of his voice and kick and thrash about. I was so grateful I'd already done up his seatbelt and he wasn't in the front seat. I had to drag him from the car into the house and he's still going strong. Nothing I tried did any good at all. He acts as though he's—"

"Demented. That's what Jo and Lou called it," Willow said, nodding. "I'll go in to him. He's my brother. Why did you take him there without me?"

She did not wait for Gram to explain. As she moved toward the door, Gram's exhausted voice came after her.

"I didn't plan it this way but I couldn't get an appointment that wasn't in school time. I thought I could surprise—"

Willow shut the door on the rest of Gram's speech. She looked down at Twig, still lying on the floor, with his arms over his face and his knees drawn up. She did not pat him or try to speak, but simply sat down on the carpet next to him and waited.

Twig cried on for another five minutes which, Willow guessed, probably felt like five hours to Gram. Twig's sister, however, could hear the storm beginning to blow over. Finally, when the little boy rolled onto his side and curled up in a ball of silent misery, she gathered him into her strong arms and, even though he tried briefly to fight her off, held him fast. His whole body shuddered against her.

"Hush, hush," she crooned into his good ear. "Willow's here. Hush, hush."

He twisted around, buried his hot, wet face in her neck and cried ordinary, tired little boy tears which did not worry her at all. Gently, she released herself—or tried to. He clung like an octopus. Then the living-room door opened and Gram came swiftly in, held out a glass of apple juice and retreated before Twig could start up again.

Smart lady, Willow thought. She's getting to know him. But she felt a deep pleasure glowing within her that her grandmother had needed her to set things to rights. Twig was still hers and he was holding onto her for all he was worth with one hand while he clutched the juice glass in the other. He drank the whole tumblerful at once. When he had finished, Willow reached out and turned on the television, flipping the channels until she felt his attention catch and the rigidity ease out of his body. She waited a couple of minutes and then dried his tears and coaxed him to blow his nose. She gave him a little more time to relax and then disengaged herself.

"I have to hang up my jacket," she said, getting up and letting him watch her shrugging out of it. "I'll be back."

He reached out, grabbed her ankle and then let his grip go loose again as the animated animals began turning cartwheels and somersaults.

Gram was sitting on the hall stairs, right outside the living-room door but hidden from Twig's sight. Her head was leaning against the wall and she had her glasses off.

"You are a magician, Willow Wind Jones," she said. "I did everything I could think of and nothing worked. How will we get him to wear the hearing aids when they come?"

"You keep telling me, 'Sufficient unto the day is the problem therein,' or whatever it is. Let's not think about that until we have to," Willow said, trying to look as though she was not one bit worried about making Twig do things.

"Yes, Mother," Gram said with a laugh. "Well, today's problem is what to have for supper. And I'd better go and see to it."

Ten days later, Gram took Twig back to get the hearing aids. Once again, the next appointment open was while Willow was at school. When Willow came dashing in from the school bus, Twig was back in front of the TV. Although he was not crying, his expression reminded her of a closed door. She was sure he knew she had come in but he would not look at her. And both hearing aids were missing.

"I don't know what he did with them," Gram said. "He snatched them out of his ears and the moment we got home he leaped out of the car and raced into the house without me. By the time I got in, they had vanished. Oh, Willow, I know I should have managed better."

Willow thought about it.

"I'll bet lots of deaf kids react this way," she said at last. "I mean, I don't like sudden changes either. Let me see what I can do. We'd better go slowly or he'll set his mind against them."

Gram kissed her.

"He's all yours," she said. "If you need me to do anything, let me know."

Willow went in and sat down as though she merely wanted to watch "Sesame Street." Twig stayed rigid and silent for another five minutes. Finally he allowed her to move closer. While they sat there, she glanced around the room. One of the couch cushions was crooked. When Twig ran to the bathroom, she dived across, and sure enough both the hearing aids were hidden there. She put them in her pocket, hoping they had not been damaged.

They were so small that he could easily have flushed them down the toilet or thrown them in the garbage. Willow was grateful he had not broken them. He was quite capable of stamping on them.

"Juice?" she suggested, rubbing his back.

He nodded. She went to get it and told Gram she had the hearing aids safe and sound.

"I have them here," Willow said, drawing them out from

her pocket. "I rescued them when he wasn't looking. I have an idea about getting him to try them."

"Good luck," said her grandmother, putting her glasses back on and blowing up at the hair that clung to her forehead. "I hope they help. She said they should make a big difference. She also said he'll need teaching from someone trained to work with deaf children."

Willow stared at her. Her dark eyes grew darker.

"Where?" she asked.

"I don't know yet. There may be a class in Kitchener. I'll find out. If there's one there, I can drive him."

Suddenly Willow felt limp. It was then she knew that she had been expecting Gram to say he would have to leave them to attend a special School for the Deaf in some faraway city. She had been prepared to fight to keep him with her but she knew it would have been awful.

Twig was subdued at supper. He kept looking from Gram to Willow and back again. He had clearly searched for the hearing aids and not found them. He was braced for the moment when one of them would try to force them into his ears.

Willow waited until he had had a long hot bath with lots of playtime. Then, when she and he were in their room, she got out her envelope of pictures with which the two of them communicated. He had reached for it but she had held the pictures out of his reach. Then she had taken one of the hearing aids and put it into her own ear. Since hers was bigger then his, it stayed in place even though it did not fit.

She stared at the first picture.

"Dog," she said.

Twig came over to see what she was up to. He looked deeply suspicious. She switched to another picture.

"Truck," she said, smiling. He loved the truck picture.

He watched her. Then he tried to snatch the picture again. She held it tight and switched.

"Baby," she said.

This time, he reached for the aid, pushed it into his ear and held out his hand for the picture she was holding. He scowled at her as he did this, so she would know he was not giving in willingly.

Willow grinned. She handed him the truck picture.

"It's a truck, Twig," she said clearly. "Truck."

"Tuck," he said.

His eyes went wide. At the sound of his own voice, magnified, with no other sounds to confuse and madden him, his interest was caught. He cocked his head on one side and held up the picture so she would say it again. She thought of making him insert the other aid and then decided to bide her time.

They went through all the pictures once. Then he reached down and tried to get his hand into her pocket. He wanted to try both. Willow, outwardly calm and inwardly turning cartwheels, got the other aid out and helped him put it in.

Then the two of them went through the pictures again. The astonishment on his face delighted her. He was actually hearing sounds he had not heard for more than two years.

After looking through the pictures yet again, he pulled the aids out and held them out to her. She accepted them without showing any anxiety and put them safely on the chest of drawers. He stared at her and then ran and got them.

"Bedtime," she told him, pointing to his bunk.

He put the aids beside his pillow and climbed in.

"Nigh," he said.

She took one of the aids, slipped it in so that he could catch sounds from it.

"Night-night, Twig," she said, stressing the "t" and then kissing him.

"Wo?" he questioned.

"Night-night," she repeated.

He wound his arms tightly around her neck and kissed her ear sloppily.

"Night-nigh', Wo," he said.

Willow managed not to gasp when she heard the "t."

Twig put the hearing aid back where he had had it, yawned, pulled his favourite blanket up to his cheek and closed his eyes. Willow sat there and waited. In less than a minute, he was asleep.

Twig could hear. Not as well as she could, but he could hear. And, even better, he could learn. And she could teach him. After all, she had already taught him so much. He wouldn't need to go to school for ages. His birthday was in January. He wouldn't be old enough for kindergarten for a long time. By the time he was ready, he would be able to talk just like other boys his age. She was sure of it.

"Night-night," she whispered again and tiptoed out of the room.

18
Just Two Little Boys

The next evening, after Twig was safely in bed, Uncle Hum invited Willow to come for a walk with him. Dusk was falling gently and the smell of violets in the grass sweetened the air. To the west the sky was still washed with gold, but in the east the first stars were pricking into view. As they set out down the drive with Sirius leading the way, Willow was tense. Had she done something wrong? Then the beauty of the evening soothed her.

Although Uncle Hum could not see the stars, he, too, was caught by the magic. He began to sing softly.

"Day is done. Gone the sun . . ."

Willow drew in a deep breath and relaxed. If she had been sure of the words, she would have joined in.

"All is well. God is nigh," Uncle Hum finished. Then, his voice still quiet, he asked her, "Willow, have you talked to Sabrina about Twig?"

Willow was so startled that she did not answer for a few seconds. They turned onto the gravel road, side by side, as she thought over what to say. At last, she settled for asking him a question in return.

"What about Twig?"

"Have you told her he has a hearing disability? Have you talked with her about your life before you came here?"

"No."

He said nothing, just let the silence grow.

"I . . . I don't know what to say. I mean, she thinks he's weird."

"Well, face it, child. You'd think he was pretty strange yourself if you knew nothing about what makes him the way he is. Are you ashamed of him?"

Willow stopped walking, anger blazing up in her.

"No, Goddamnit!" she yelled. "Of course not. Why should I be? I love him. He's my brother."

Uncle Hum amazed her by chuckling.

"Con's my sister and I love her but I have to admit I find myself embarrassed by her often," he said. "I think you owe it to your brother to talk openly about his disabilities and abilities. Matthew Marr and he might be friends. He needs children to play with, you know. You've been his mother and his teacher and his rock, all rolled into one. You'll always be closer to him than anyone else, I think, but everybody needs more than one other person."

Silence came again as Willow struggled with her muddled feelings. At last, she said feebly, "How will I begin?"

"Just plunge in. If you stick to the truth, you can't go wrong. I suspect rumours will be winging around Ponsonby

School about your brother and it's always best to scotch a rumour before it's loose and there's no catching up with it. We could talk a bit about what you might say, if you like?"

Willow nodded and then remembered he couldn't see.

"Yes," she said hurriedly. "I don't know how much to tell."

"What matters is that he has a severe hearing loss in one ear and a moderate loss in the other. He is also ADHD, we think. It means Attention Deficit Hyperactivity Disorder."

"What?" Willow interrupted, startled. "Say that again. Slowly."

Uncle Hum did and went on to explain.

"It's why he has trouble sitting still, has difficulty focusing his attention on things in which he isn't intensely interested. It's why he finds it very hard switching from one activity to another."

"Why is he like that? Is it . . . Was it the drugs?"

"Probably. You were born before your mother got hooked but Twig spent eleven months dependent on drugs."

"Eleven months . . . "

"When he was in the womb, every time she had a fix, so did he. If she hallucinated, he shared it somehow. If she was zonked, he was too. Then, after his birth, you yourself told Nell that Lou gave him something to get him through the time of withdrawal."

"Yes," Willow said, her voice so low he stopped walking to hear her. The memory of those early days with her brother made her shiver even though it was a mild evening.

"It may not have been the drugs," he went on when she did not speak. "Sometimes it just happens for no known reason. Twig's frustration with his struggles sets him screaming sometimes. I'm sure the Marrs have heard him once in a while and been anxious. To tell the truth, that's what set me on to talk this over with you. Sabrina's mother inquired, ever so hesitantly, what was wrong with the little boy when Sirius and I went over to get eggs. She knew we couldn't be abusing him but she'd never heard such a prolonged rumpus, I guess."

Willow went stiff with fury and then forced herself to relax. If she had lived next door, she'd have wondered too. So Sabrina must be dying of curiosity. She'd done well to keep quiet this long. It must be killing her.

Uncle Hum laughed. "I can feel you wanting to screech yourself," he said. "But curiosity is an admirable trait really. The thing you must do is open up to Sabrina and do your best to keep calm while you're doing it. It's nothing to be ashamed of; it's something to be understood. My blindness is like Twig's deafness. We have nothing to be ashamed of but we both need special help sometimes. As he gets older, you'll have to help him know how to tell people about himself."

They went on talking even after they were home again, until Willow felt she could handle discussing her brother calmly. She even knew it would be a relief. She had kept it all bottled up for so long. And, she knew, her silence about it was beginning to rub on her friendship with Sabrina.

I'll do it tomorrow, she promised herself. I'll start with Matthew.

The following afternoon, Willow saw Gram and Twig waiting for the bus. They looked far from happy. She scrambled down the steps, came around in front of the bus and crossed the road to them. Twig rushed at her, hugging her much harder than usual and giving Gram a look of deep dislike over his shoulder.

What now? Willow thought wearily, stooping to hug him back.

"Do you suppose you could stay outside with him for a while?" Gram asked. "Con is livid with rage at him. He cut off all the long hair on Panda's tail. We caught him as he was starting on Toby. He nicked him slightly so the dog yipped, of course. Con is convinced that next time he gets hold of a weapon he'll murder us all in our beds."

She gave a snort of laughter as she repeated her sister's words but Willow was not deceived. Gram was tired out by Twig and worried by him. She pictured Panda with a skinny little hairless tail and she herself felt sick.

"I'll keep him with me," she promised. "I might kill him myself."

"We could go on a hike down by the creek," Sabrina suggested, clearly believing she was included in the party.

Willow had forgotten Sabrina was there until she spoke. She looked at her and said, "Okay. But only if you go home and bring your little brother too."

"Matthew?" Sabrina said, her look startled, shocked even.

"Do you have any other little brothers?" Willow asked, her voice as sharp as Aunt Con's. "Twig never gets to play with other boys. He's a human boy, you know. He's not some rare species."

"But Matthew isn't . . . I mean, he's . . . "

"Get him, Sabrina, or get lost," Willow ground out through clenched teeth. "We'll wait."

This was not the way she had intended to start. Uncle Hum had told her to keep calm. But she hated people talking about Twig as though he were some sort of freak, dangerous to sweet little "normal" boys like Matthew Marr.

Sabrina, flustered and confused, turned on her heel and headed off on the beaten path the two of them had created between their houses. Then she stopped dead. She was staring back at the garage. Willow turned to see what had caught her attention. Then she stared too.

While she and Sabrina had been talking, Twig had taken off without waiting for them. Now the two girls gazed, mouths agape, at two little boys who were jabbering away at each other and climbing on the woodpile by the garage. It was as clear as crystal that they had played together before, that they knew each other very well and took their differences entirely for granted. Twig's words, which Willow had believed she alone understood, were proving no problem to Matthew and Twig kept looking at the other boy and nodding his head when Matthew yelled commands.

Willow was stunned. How long had the boys been playing? She had believed she knew everything about her brother but she had been so wrong. Suddenly she took in what it meant. She was not going to have to help Twig learn to play with other children. He knew. She was not going to have to protect him from Sabrina. Sabrina couldn't help seeing how much fun Matthew was having with him.

She started toward Sabrina, who was standing stock-still, her wide eyes fixed on the joyous, busy children.

"They already know each other," Willow said.

"Yeah. They sure do. And Matthew . . . he understands

Twig perfectly. It's amazing," Sabrina said in a disbelieving voice.

"Maybe not so amazing," Willow said as they strolled, side by side, toward the woodpile. "After all, they're both little kids. Twig has trouble hearing . . . "

"Is that all it is?" Sabrina exclaimed, stopping to look at Willow. "I thought he was retarded . . . "

"I know you did. But I don't think he's mentally handi-capped," Willow said, hearing herself sounding stuffy. She kept going all the same. "But suppose he is? As long as Matthew doesn't care, why should you? He's still just a little boy."

"It's the screams," Sabrina mumbled, studying the toe of her boot. "We can hear him all the way over at our place. Matt yells too, but never like that."

Willow was silenced for a moment. She knew Sabrina was only speaking the truth. Sunny little Matthew, beloved by his family and everyone else in sight, had no need to scream. She did not want to tell the other girl about her mother's drug addiction nor about Lou's brother nor about any of the tough things in her past life that still haunted her dreams. But she would have to make some explanation. The Marrs were wondering.

"Are you a blabbermouth?" The question popped out before she could catch it back. She knew the answer. Sabrina could have told her lots of stuff about her big sisters or the other kids in their class but she never had. Willow blushed.

"I'm sorry . ... " she started.

"I do not blab," Sabrina said loftily. Then she began to laugh.

The woodpile had begun to come apart under the boys' booted feet. With shrieks of glee, they were leaping from log to log as the chunks of wood came loose and rolled down.

"Twig, watch out!" Willow yelled, even though he would not hear her. At the same instant, she leaped to rescue him.

He did not want rescuing. He and Matthew, ignoring their precarious footing, were joyously scrambling up on the end of the pile they had yet to topple.

"They're okay," Sabrina assured her. "It's not as though your grandmother has an enormous woodpile like the Chathams."

Willow was thankful. The Chathams heated their house and cooked all their food on woodstoves. Their pile looked as big as a log cabin.

The laughter was like a healing wind. Willow turned to face Sabrina and started talking. She had never confided anything in another girl her own age before. It felt wonderful. Sabrina's ready sympathy was balm. She was also awed by what Willow had to say. She was shocked, too, and angry when she heard about Lou's brother and Maisie and Sergeant Evans. Willow left out stuff about her mother. Sabrina did not have to know everything. "So now you know," she finished off. "Let's get those baboons busy piling the wood up again. They made the mess; they should help fix it."

If she meant to punish the two little boys, it did not work. They loved stacking the wood. They were bursting with pride as they fetched fat chunky logs to their sisters, who stood on the pile and placed each one securely. They thought they were grown up. They saw themselves as men.

Willow did not notice that Twig was not wearing his

hearing aids until Gram called them to come in and wash
their hands for supper. Then she decided not to say anything
until they had finished eating. As she helped take out the
bread pudding bowls, she asked, "Twig's hearing aids . . . ?"

"Wait. We'll talk after he's asleep," her grandmother said.

Waiting was hard but getting Twig upstairs and into the
bathtub kept her occupied. Then getting him out again was
no mean feat and settling him took ages. He was still excited
about his adventures on the woodpile.

Willow finally got him settled and ran lightly down to
where Gram sat waiting.

"Don't look so worried, child," her grandmother said. "It's
just that Smithson School in Kitchener has agreed to take
him and I thought we could let it ride until he sees other children wearing them too."

Willow wanted to throw herself down on the carpet and
scream like Twig. Why had she never even heard of Smithson
School? Who did Gram think she was anyway? How dare she
make plans for Twig as though his sister had nothing to say?
Willow had seen him born and cared for him for three,
almost four, years. He was hers, not Gram's.

She opened her mouth to tell her grandmother, once and
for all, that she was not the one in charge of Twig. She knew
exactly what to say, how to start anyway. "You aren't even his
blood relation . . . "

"Willow, wait. Don't start telling me off until you've
heard the rest. I've arranged for you to come along," Gram
said, smiling at her granddaughter's furious expression. "I
phoned Ponsonby and explained. You'll know best whether it
is the right place for him. They told me most of the children

203

who come there start when they're three. It's an oral method. They'll teach him to lip-read and build on the speech he has."

Willow sank down on the nearest chair.

"What if he hates it?" she whispered, not looking at Gram.

"We'll think again. It's a trial run. You and I and his teacher will get together to decide what's best."

"I'll be there?"

"Of course," Gram said, a note of impatience sharpening her voice. "He's your boy, Willow, even though that's a tall order for a girl your age. Nobody knows him as well as you and no one else can handle him the way you do."

"I don't mind," Willow got out, feeling like a punctured balloon and, at the same time, like a balloon floating joyously up into the sky.

Gram reached out and put both arms around her and hugged her close, pulling her onto her lap as though she were Twig's size.

"I do love you, Willow Wind Jones," she said into her granddaughter's ear. "More than a bushel and a peck."

Willow snorted.

"You're going to have to study up," she said. "Canada went metric years ago."

Then she pulled herself free and started looking through the pile of videos.

"Homework," Gram said firmly.

"But if I'm not going to school tomorrow . . . " Willow tried.

"I love you a kilo and a litre," Gram said, "but you still have homework to do."

19
Twig Starts School

Twig hung back as they entered the classroom. He even put his thumb in his mouth for a minute and held on tight to the edge of Willow's vest.

"Here. Sit down," the teacher said. "Let's just give him a few moments to look us over before we try to include him. His name is Twig? Is that right?"

Gram looked at Willow and waited. Willow had known this was coming.

"His nickname is Twig," she said. "His real name is Cal. I think he should be called Cal at school."

"Short for Calvin?" the teacher asked.

"Maybe," Willow muttered. "But don't call him Calvin. Just Cal. I've told him."

"Well, well," Gram said. "You have been busy."

Willow shot her a sideways look.

"Just preparing him," she said. "You said he needed to be prepared."

"You know what," Gram said to the teacher, "if I were you, I'd call him Twig at first. He has a lot to assimilate . . . "

Twig had removed his thumb from his mouth and taken a hesitant step toward the four children who were seated in a semicircle. There was an empty chair. He eyed it.

Willow stood up and took his hand. It was moist with sweat. She led him gently forward.

"This is your chair, Twig," she said.

Twig pulled away slightly but he didn't mean it. Graham, the boy sitting in the chair next to the empty one, thumped it with his fist and beckoned. Nobody else moved.

Then, very slowly, Twig edged close enough for Graham to pull him into it with a loud laugh. Twig stiffened, met Graham's merry eyes and grinned sheepishly.

Willow, as softly as though she were wearing velvet slippers, stole back to sit next to her grandmother.

Graham did not look at all like Patrick but he reminded her of him. Patrick had helped her find her way at Ponsonby whenever Sabrina forgot or failed to realize how lost she was feeling. It turned out that he had only lived in Canada since he was eight and he remembered how it felt not only to look different but to start in the spring instead of the fall.

"Go with the flow, Tree," he said.

All the boys and some of the girls called her Tree now and, to her own surprise, she liked it.

"Patrick's nice," she told Sabrina.

"He's okay," Sabrina said off-handedly.

Willow, seeing her friend's eyes narrowing, let the subject rest. But she herself found it deeply satisfying to have not one but two friends. For a girl who had never had one, two seemed like a crowd.

Gram and the two children stayed for the morning at Twig's school and then, much to Graham's disgust, went home early. Twig fell asleep when they were only halfway.

"Are you ready to give your verdict?" Gram asked.

"I think he likes it there," Willow said slowly. "He'll like going. He already has a friend."

"Just what I thought," her grandmother said. "We'll give it a month or so and see."

"They weren't learning sign language," Willow said uncertainly.

"If he was profoundly deaf, we'd have taken that route. There's a school in Milton. But I thought we'd start this way."

"Some of the kids talked on their hands when she wasn't looking," Willow observed. "He'll soon pick it up. I saw a program about sign language on TV. It sounded neat. It sounded . . . important."

"We'll get to it if we decide that's what he needs. You and I could learn it too maybe. But it won't help him communicate with Hum."

Willow had not thought of that. If—when—Twig learned to read though, he and Uncle Hum would have it made.

That afternoon, Gram took Aunt Con to have her cast removed. Everyone was glad she was mobile again. The little dogs frisked around her, ecstatic to find her restored to them. They looked meaningfully at their leashes. Aunt Con laughed.

"Not yet," she said. "You have the whole backyard fenced in. Go dash about out there."

Willow looked to see if Panda's tail was returning to its former snowy plume. It was beginning to. And now that Twig had school all day and Matthew to play with when he got home, he wouldn't be giving dogs haircuts. He might come up with something worse, of course, but not for a week or two.

He loved school. Gram drove him at first but it turned out that the school board would pay for him to be picked up since he was what was called a Special Needs Child. Gram had said she didn't mind but she, too, was relieved not to have to run a daily delivery service.

"I felt a little like a yo-yo," she admitted. "Back and forth, back and forth. Of course, it's a price you pay for living in the country. Do you ever wish we lived in town, Willow?"

"Never," Willow said.

She thought for an instant of Maisie's building and then pushed the memory away. She was here and she was safe and so was Twig. It was going to stay that way.

Just in case, she reached out and knocked her knuckles against the nearest wooden bookshelf.

By now, Willow had read her birthday copy of Elspet Gordon's story. Uncle Hum had put it on disk and offered to print it out for her but she felt closer to the girl who had lived so long ago when she puzzled out Elspet's faded handwriting. She had not told anyone but she was quite sure that she had seen Elspet two or three times since she and Twig had come to Ontario. It was always a glimpse only and she always came when Willow was worried or lonely. Afterwards, Willow felt comforted somehow. Unless, of course, she was imagining the entire thing.

The uncertainty about what would happen to Aunt Con now cast the only shadow in the sunny house. She still made Willow mad often with her tactless remarks, her quick temper and her frequent demands for service. But she was part of the family and Willow could not imagine Stonecrop without her and her darling boys. Willow knew Gram got fed up with her sister daily, and sometimes Uncle Hum did too but nobody now spoke of her leaving. Even though their silence was a relief, it settled nothing. Willow was sure Aunt Con still lay awake nights worrying. Knowing how this felt, Willow decided it was up to her to make them all come out into the open.

"Gram, why don't you tell Aunt Con she can stay?" she blurted out one afternoon when they were alone in the garden.

"I keep hoping she'll make other arrangements," Gram said, after a long silent moment.

"You know she won't. I think you just can't be bothered. She's kinfolks," Willow said, remembering Maisie's words. "She needs us."

"All she has to do is say so," Gram snapped. She stubbornly kept her back turned. Watching that stiff back, Willow knew she ought to let the subject drop and try again later.

The next day was Sunday. Gram took Willow to church with her in the morning while Uncle Hum kept Twig from wrecking the house or tormenting the animals. Leaving him was growing easier. Willow was not actively worried about him any longer as she sat in the pew beside her grandmother. She half-listened to the minister telling the younger children what God was like. She began by asking them for suggestions.

"He's a big man on a cloud," one of the five-year-olds announced. "And he yells at you like my Grandpa."

Everyone chuckled as the minister began to set the kid straight.

"God is a Spirit," she said. "You cannot see God. But God is always there when you need a friend, ready to listen, ready to comfort you, ready to give you strength."

Like Red Mouse, Willow thought, grinning.

The minister went on about God being all powerful, all knowing, just, merciful, full of loving kindness . . .

Willow tuned her out. She didn't need that big, heavy God. He had not helped her while she and Twig were alone with Jake or when they were cold and hungry at Maisie's.

I'll just keep Red Mouse, she thought.

Good thinking, Red Mouse remarked. I was afraid, for a second, that you were going to suggest I retire.

The house and its inhabitants were peaceful as they drove up. Uncle Hum had made something he called Dish, made by throwing tins of practically everything into a deep frying pan and heating it up. Everyone liked it but Twig, who had hot dogs. As she stood up to clear away the bowls, Willow heard her great-aunt, with no warning, burst out into loud speech.

"I have to tell you something," she started.

Willow had been about to join Twig at the TV when she felt her great-aunt's hand reach out and grasp hers. It was as though she were the adult, Aunt Con the child. She returned the squeeze, sat down and waited.

Then Aunt Con told the other adults what Willow had guessed. She was not really sick; she was broke. It was a long story and her cheeks were flushed and she was out of breath at the finish.

"So, unless you want to see me on welfare, I can't leave," she said. "I want to stay here. I've come to love these children, even that rascal Twig. But I know you don't want me . . . "

Her voice cracked and she clutched Willow's hand hard. Gram shot a look at Uncle Hum. Then she laughed.

"We've known your situation for some time, Con," she said quietly. "Of course, you must stay with us. By now, much as I hate to admit it, we'd miss you and your boys with their butterfly ears. I would have thrown you out if you'd insisted on my grandchildren leaving but, since you've come to your senses, we'll do our best to put up with you. You might even be helpful."

Willow would once have thought her grandmother was mean but she knew her better now. And she knew exactly what was about to happen.

Aunt Con burst into tears. Uncle Hum laughed and cleared his throat. And Gram got up and hugged her sister.

"Better the devil you know than the devil you don't," she said.

Willow left them to it. She had promised Sabrina to spend the afternoon working on their nature project down by Cox's Creek. Twig, of course, came after her. But she didn't mind.

"Better the devil you know," she murmured. "Okay, Twig. You can come."

"Cal," Twig said softly. "Cal."

20
Gram's Decision

Summer arrived before the end of May. In June, despite the bugs, Gram was forever disappearing into the garden. Aunt Con did the watering in the evening but she absolutely refused to get down on her knees and "grovel over a bunch of weeds." Uncle Hum claimed he could not see well enough to pull weeds or direct a hose and sat on the back porch and listened to Willow and Twig and their friends playing.

"Are you lonely?" Willow asked him.

"I've always got Red Mouse," he said.

Willow shook her head even though she knew he wouldn't see. Red Mouse was hers.

"You can have his sisters," she offered.

"Thank you so much," he said lazily and went on swinging gently in his hammock chair. She would have felt sorry for him if she had not seen, by the faraway look in his unfocussed eyes, that he was writing inside his head. You could always tell.

She went through the back gate and started toward the garden. She was beginning to enjoy gardening even though she pretended to be doing Gram a big favour by helping.

Red Mouse, she said.

Red Mouse did not answer. Willow's feet slowed as she waited. Then she heard a chuckle. Red Mouse was there . . . or was it Uncle Hum? Or Gram? She tried to concentrate, panic rising inside her.

Don't fret. You can't get rid of your resident rodent, said the familiar, teasing voice.

Willow grinned. Even though she didn't need to consult him every other minute now, she still needed to know he was there.

"Are you coming to lend a hand?" Gram called. "How about picking some berries before the birds get them all?"

"If you'll make shortcake for supper," Willow said, turning back to fetch the bowl.

When Willow sat down that evening to tackle her homework, the phone rang before she had found her place in the math text. Hoping it was Sabrina, she shut the book again, pushed back her chair and lifted the receiver. She did this gently so as not to interrupt a call intended for Gram but was still stunned by the words she overheard her grandmother uttering.

"Ms Thornton, thanks for getting back to me. I need to talk with you about plans for the children's future. We can't let things drift on this way. I managed to reach my daughter yesterday . . . "

Willow hung up with only a faint click, although her hand was trembling. Then she sank onto the nearest chair and struggled to understand what she had heard her grandmother say. Gram had spoken to Angel. She had not told Willow, so it must be that she had not wanted Willow to know. Now she was getting Ms Thornton in on whatever she was planning. It was something to do with herself and Twig. Ms Thornton found foster home placements for kids. Why would Gram be asking her for help?

Foster homes . . . foster homes . . . foster . . . The two words rang on and on in Willow's head like axe blows cutting at the trunk of a living tree. Over and over and over they struck. And they let a terrible cold come into her.

No, Gram, she whispered. No. Not now.

Then she thrust the terror away from her. She had believed Angel's words about Gram before and they had been lies. Even though she had heard these words with her own ears, there must be some other explanation. Gram would not have found a school for Twig if she planned to send him away. She had talked of the two of them working together to help him with language. How could they do that if they weren't together? Surely Willow must have misunderstood.

But what else could it mean? If they were staying at Stonecrop, why would her grandmother have called Ms Thornton?

And Angel, whispered another voice. She spoke to Angel. She didn't tell me.

Willow stood up. She would march right up those stairs to Gram and ask her right out, face to face, what was going on.

She tried to but her feet would not move.

Aunt Con came in. She stared at Willow.

"What is it, child? You look as though you'd been turned to stone."

"I'm not stone," Willow got out.

Stones did not feel like this, torn apart, so afraid. Stones had it easy. Moving like a wind-up toy, Willow returned to her math homework and made sure every answer was correct. She got through the rest of the evening somehow. She made it through the following day too, although Sabrina asked her a couple of times what was wrong.

In spite of the perfect homework, she nearly failed the surprise math test, but it didn't matter. School would soon be finished for the summer.

When Gram wants to do something, Willow thought at one point, she never asks other people. She just goes ahead full blast. Willow could still hear clearly her grandmother's voice saying, "Of course you can come. Twig too." She really should have discussed it with Uncle Hum first but she hadn't.

I trust her, she told herself. She loves us. I will trust her.

But it was almost more than she could manage.

They had another strawberry shortcake for supper but Willow could not taste it. After Twig was asleep, she put her own pajamas on without being told and got into bed herself.

If she and Twig had to run, where could they go?

Gram discovered her in her bed.

"My heavens, child," she said, sounding surprised but not as though she had her mind on it. "Come on into my room. We have things to talk over."

Feeling sick at her stomach, Willow trailed after her. Gram

was so full of what she herself wanted to say that she didn't notice how tense her granddaughter was. Willow listened stonily, unable to take in the first few words Gram said to her. When they began to make sense, however, her heart unclenched and reached out gratefully for the fine, strong truth.

"Ms Thornton and I have been talking. I didn't tell you until I had some definite news. I have made application to get legal custody of both you and Twig. I should have done it years ago. Then Angel would not have been able to take you the way she did. It won't change much around here except you will know you are safe. You will be officially my children."

"Oh, Gram," was all Willow could squeeze past the tightness in her throat.

"They say there will be no problem. I actually managed to reach your mother and she has agreed. Ms Thornton told me to tell Hum that his being the author of the Red Mouse books helped. Since you were the one who made up that mouse in the beginning, I thought you'd be pleased."

I try to do my little part, Red Mouse drawled.

Willow could not think what to say so she just gave Gram a strangling hug and a fast kiss. Kissing made her nervous even now. The embrace loosed her tongue and she told Gram she had overheard her talking to Ms Thornton.

"Oh, Willow," Gram said.

"But I trusted you," Willow put in hastily. She did not bother to explain how hard that had been to do.

Gram hugged her and started to sing about loving her "a bushel and a peck."

"Gram, I've told you to catch up with the times," Willow teased. "Canada has gone metric."

Gram instantly began to sing a revised version.

> *I love you a kilo and a litre.*
> *Nowhere have I ever met*
> *A little girl who's sweeter . . .*

She trailed off, laughing at herself. Willow, leaning against her, thought hard and fast. After a couple of minutes, she began to sing herself.

> *I love you a gallon and a quart.*
> *I love you pounds and ounces too,*
> *Because you're such a sport.*
> *Very, very fond of you*
> *Is what I truly am.*
> *Sweeter than a metre or a litre is*
> *My Gram.*

Uncle Hum applauded from the hallway and then asked if his sisters would like to take on himself and Willow in a game of cribbage. Willow, who had learned to love the game, did not mention that she had gone to bed already.

"Sure," she said, jumping up.

She found the game comforting. In the first hand, she got a double double run plus the right jack.

"Way to go, niece," Uncle Hum exulted.

Moving their peg seventeen holes cheered her. As the play continued, though, she could not help thinking about the fact that Angel, without once speaking to them, had agreed to sign papers giving her and her brother away. It shouldn't matter. She and Twig would be safe. It was what she had wanted most in the world. And they were more than just safe; they were loved. She swallowed hard and blinked away the mist that blurred the cards she held.

"Thirty," Aunt Con said.

Willow had stopped listening.

"Is it a 'go,' Willow?" her aunt demanded, reaching for her peg.

"Thirty-one," Willow said and put down her ace.

21
Journey Map

A week later, when Willow got off the bus, nobody was home. Twig had not yet arrived. Gram and Aunt Con were in town shopping. They had told her they would not be home. Uncle Hum and Sirius were out for a walk. She had seen them through the bus window. The Marrs had gone visiting relatives in Toronto. Sabrina had been picked up at school.

For the first time since Twig's birth, Willow Wind Jones was totally on her own. She walked down the lane slowly, listening to the birds singing, looking up at the fat clouds sailing across the blue sky, drinking in the garden smells from the manure across the road to the fringe tree blooming by the front door. It felt as though the world had just been created for her to revel in. She heard the dogs barking but the noise didn't bother her. They were only welcoming her home.

She opened the front door and threw her backpack in,

knowing but not caring that Gram would be after her to hang it up the moment she arrived.

Crocus strolled around the corner of the house and meowed. Willow stooped to stroke him.

"I'm going to climb the willow tree," she announced.

Crocus meandered away, waving his tail. He knew when petting time was over. He'd already climbed that tree.

Willow ran to the tree and began to climb. There were a few helpful steps nailed to the trunk and then she was up in the swinging branches. She usually had Twig or Sabrina or even Matthew right behind her and had to watch out not to kick them, but not now. When she was as far up as it was safe to go, she perched there, gazing around, feeling like an explorer who had stumbled on an undiscovered land.

"I will be your queen," she told the bees and birds, the caterpillars, the spring peepers and Crocus. If she sounded foolish, none of them laughed. It sounded wonderfully majestic to Willow's ears.

She could see the stretch of grass Matthew Marr called the Millions of Grass Meadow, the Tree Trap from which she had had to rescue both boys, the pond which Gram called Golden Fish Pond, the clump of shadowy trees she had, secretly, dubbed the Deep Dark Forest, and her own apple tree, which had no name yet because nothing she could think of was lovely enough.

"A map," she cried suddenly. Then, more quietly, "I'll make a map."

She was on her way down the willow when she remembered the sheet of paper she had seen littering the playground and stuffed in her hip pocket. She winkled it out, found a stub of pencil in her shoe and began. It was a smallish, grubby map but she could do it properly later. Twig would be home soon. She had to hurry. He would not understand map-making.

She pencilled in the creek at the foot of the long hill and then added the bridge even though it was not strictly part of their property. It was also only a flat bridge, not one that soared up and had railings. But it should have a name. She had christened almost everything else. She paused to think about bridge names and remembered the song Angel had sung. It seemed such a long time ago now, a lifetime almost. Back then she had thought that she and Twig were like two children trapped in the deep, rushing water under a high bridge.

Well, they had escaped. They had come through the Dark Forest sitting in the police station and then, helped by Ms Thornton and Star, they had . . . they had climbed on a friendly dragon who had flown them through the night to the safety of Stonecrop.

I could make a map of that journey, Twig's and my quest for a home. Maybe. Or a story.

If she did, where were they now? Not Oz or Narnia or Middle Earth or Prydain or Terabithia. Did Stonecrop sound like a magical country? Maybe. She could figure it out as she drew it. A journey map. She could end it with them arriving at the Land of Stonecrop and then make another map of their new country. Because they really weren't at the end. They were still just beginning.

Inside the house, the phone rang.

She almost stayed where she was and let it go unanswered.

The person would be sure to leave Gram a message. But what if something had happened to Twig?

Willow swung down like Tarzan, or Jane, and landed on the grass on her hands and knees. Scrambling to her feet, she ran for the house. Just before she got there, the ringing stopped, but after only a few seconds it began again.

"Hello," Willow gasped, trying to catch her breath and go on thinking of her journey map.

Silence.

"Hello," Willow said again, snapping to attention and raising her voice slightly.

"Willow? Is that you?"

"Yes," Willow said blankly. Then, in the next second, she knew who it was. The husky, so familiar voice sounded far, far away.

"Willow, it's me. Angel. Mum, I mean."

"I know," Willow said. She could feel her whole body beginning to shake. She gripped the receiver with one hand and the edge of the kitchen table with the other. She had longed for Angel to phone. Why was she so afraid? And why couldn't she think of anything to say?

Silence again.

"Willow, are you still there?"

"I'm still here. Where are you? Have you been trying to find us?"

"I met Ms Thornton a while ago and she told me to call Star. Then Mum called last week and they brought me papers to sign. Are you all right? How's my baby?"

"He's no baby," Willow said, her heart hardening against the woman who had left Twig where he could be hurt.

JourneyMap

"Cal's going to school. He's in a special class for deaf kids."

"What? Did you say 'Cal'? Who's Cal?"

"Your baby. The one you named Calypso. They call him Cal. They think it's short for Calvin. I let them."

Angel laughed. The laugh was tired but it was the laugh Willow had loved ever since she could remember. Deep, throaty, with a warmth that made her want to cry.

"Willow, one of these days I promise things will get better . . . " the weary voice said. "I signed the papers, but someday . . . "

Willow held the phone away from herself for a moment. Her mother was crying. She would not let Angel guess she was in tears too. She scrubbed them away with the heel of her hand and spoke into the receiver.

"You don't need to promise. It was right to sign. We're fine here. Gram is great and so is Uncle Hum. They take good care of us. And Aunt Con does too."

"Aunt Con! My God, she hated Star and me when we were teenagers. She's a racist." Angel's voice rose and then died away.

Willow could not take any more. She did not want to have to explain about Aunt Con. She saw again, in her mind's eye, the picture Gram had of Angel at sixteen. The beautiful face was sulky, heavily made up and sporting a nose ring. The shirt was too low, too tight and too slinky. That Angel must have driven Aunt Con crazy.

Willow could not tell her mother Aunt Con was bankrupt. Angel would be too pleased.

Willow found herself gulping in air as though she had been running. She needed to get away.

"Mum, I love you," she said in as steady a voice as she could manage. "But Cal's taxi is going to pull up and I want to be outside to meet him. Do you need me to tell Gram something?"

"No," her mother whispered. "I mean, yes . . . Tell her I love her. I know she will love you both. She always loved Star and me, no matter what. You do what she tells you, do you hear?"

"Yes."

"Willow . . . "

"Yes," Willow said again.

"Kiss Twig for me . . . "

"Cal," Willow said and waited, hoping Angel would laugh once more.

But, far away in Vancouver, the receiver clicked into its cradle. Willow Jones held onto hers a moment longer. Then she, too, hung up. She wished Gram had been home.

I'm back under the bridge, she thought dully.

No, you are not, Red Mouse said, his words clear, strong and comforting. Not unless you choose to be.

She did not so choose. She refused to return to that sad, lonely place. Red Mouse was right. She shook off the shadows that Angel's sadness cast. She pushed herself out into the light, taking her brother with her. Inside her head, she pictured the two of them clambering up an embankment and reaching the safety of the bridge. She and Twig would always remember being afraid but they had now climbed to freedom and they had people to hold onto.

Kinfolks.

She ran outside again and stood in the sunny summer

afternoon. Crocus arrived, purring, as if he sensed her need of him, and she scooped him up and held his furry body tight.

Let me go, Angel, she thought. You'll have to let us both go.

And as she stood there, filled to the brim with fear and freedom and a wrenching love, she saw the taxi with Twig inside turn down the lane.

"Cal!" she yelled and, still hugging a rumpled tabby cat, raced to meet him. By the time she got there, Crocus had had enough. He sprang out of her grip and streaked away to the backyard. Far up the road, she could see the van rocketing along with Gram driving hell-bent-for-leather. She had said she would try to beat Twig home and she had almost done it.

Willow laughed and opened the rear door for her brother. She thanked the driver while Twig undid his seatbelt. Grabbing his backpack, he slid out and grinned up at her.

"Let's play tag, Calypso Jones," she said.

He did a little dance. Then he dropped his backpack on the driveway.

"Okay, Wiyo," said Twig. "You It."